CW00350843

A Shark in the Bath
And Other Stories

John Reid Young

Cover and Illustrations

By

Annie Chapman

Copyright © 2018 John Reid Young

All rights reserved.

ISBN:
ISBN-13: 978-84-697-6160-1

For Beatriz, William and Oliver.

CONTENTS

Acknowledgments   i

1   The Man from La Guancha   1

2   A Shark in the Bath   34

3   Two Witches and a Fortune   55

4   The Yoyo and the Buddha   79

5   Illegal Immigrant   96

6   A Missed Call   121

7   Under the Waterfall   145

8   Innocent Scoundrel   173

PUBLISHER'S NOTE

These short stories are fictional. Although some of the names which appear belong to members of the author's family and ancestors other characters and names are either the product of the author's imagination or are used fictitiously. Any resemblance to actual persons, living or dead, is entirely coincidental

ACKNOWLEDGMENTS

I would specially like to thank Annie Chapman, once again, for her wonderful illustrations. Her pencil and colours add such flavour to my stories.

I am eternally grateful to Julia Baillon, whose reading eye and magic marmalades I could not have done without.

My thanks also go to Agustín Guimerá, Ken Fisher, Joe Cawley and so many other friends for their enthusiasm and support.

THE MAN FROM LA GUANCHA

It is unusual to find young travellers to the Canary Islands leaving the luxury of their all-inclusive hotels or sun-tanning beach. Some only feel at home if they don't wander off too far away from the resort's happy-hour pub ambience.

But a different, more adventurous breed does exist. They like to devour the delicacies of indigenous cuisine. They seek out the island's hidden charms. They want to bathe in rock pools and chase sunsets through the pine forests and over volcanic landscapes. They discover the idiosyncrasy of mountain villages. Albeit without the danger that accompanied early adventurers they do much as their ancestors did before the invention of modern tourism.

One of these is Alex Marriot and in September 2016 he decided to take his new girlfriend for a week's holiday on the island of Tenerife.

Alex, an American by birth, had returned to live in the land of his ancestors in the English countryside after a period reading Archaeology and Anthropology at Oxford University. A brilliant student, he had been offered a contract as a field archaeologist by rival Cambridge University. His aim, however, was to start work on a doctorate soon after this short holiday.

Whilst searching for options he came across something about an ancient pre-Hispanic nation inhabiting the Canary Islands. It caught his anthropological imagination.

A holiday in Tenerife made sense. It was a short distance away by plane. It had beaches and promised sun. It appeared to possess an interesting culture and a unique history which he might pursue. It was also a favourite destination for European travel companies. However, instead of plunging for a magnificent, luxury hotel on a white-sand beach, Alex and Sophie chose to book something more exotic which they found browsing through websites and which offered rooms away from the masses.

They were not disappointed when their hired car and GPS finally took them to an address on the edge of a banana plantation. The key to the gate was under an upturned, terracotta flower pot beneath the bougainvillea, just as the man had said it would be, and the evening light shone enough for them to make their way to the small, reception room. They found another key and instructions waiting for them on an antique table which was adorned with a vase of wild lavender.

The *Hacienda de Las Cuatro Ventanas* was that kind of place and its owners were those kind of people. The 17th century Canary Island house on the edge of the banana plantation had been beautifully restored to provide self-catering accommodation for adventurous or privacy-seeking travellers. It's thick, stone walls were hidden below the main northwest road, under steep cliffs and just above a black sand beach called *El Socorro*. It advertised luxury rooms and was described as a property designed to respect the rich, natural and historic heritage of old colonial life.

Dawn and sunset were a view of the ocean through ferns and mango trees. For company they had two German couples who came and went as silently as the bats. The only sounds were those of water gurgling down an aqueduct beside the banana plantation, geckoes laughing at each other in the night and the kestrels calling as they hovered in search of lizards or mice.

The plan was to explore as much of the island as possible but Alex had promised Sophie a lazy first day on the beach. By the middle of the morning they were already watching the first surfers darting along the unfolding waves of *El Socorro*.

The *chiringuito* under the cliff was a welcome refuge from the mid-day sun and for a taste of seafood and a chilled local *Dorada* beer.

"Hey, look at that!" said Alex pointing skywards.

There were three paragliders, yellow, blue and pink and they circled over the tips of the waves before gliding in, like giant sea eagles, to perfect landings on the sand.

Alex began to wish they had not seen them. One of them carried two people, an instructor and a passenger.

"Oh, I must try that. Can we?" pleaded Sophie excitedly.

She was quite the opposite to her patient, gentle, anthropologist lover. Sophie was very get-up-and-go. In winter she was an avid skier. At weekends she went rock-climbing when she wasn't playing for the local hockey team. But nothing got her going more than trying something new, dangerous and sometimes shocking. Even as a lover she was the eager explorer whilst Alex was the prudent. For lunch she had asked to try some grilled limpets recently prised off the rocks. Alex Marriot was just brave enough to go for a red sea bream with wrinkled potatoes.

The name on the silver and grey van was *Ibrafly*. Ibrahim is a master of the skies in Tenerife and an experienced instructor. He has flown and spun in the sky with the best paragliders in Europe. Like many a professional with a mission to accomplish Ibrahim is not the greatest talker. He gave Alex a card and told him he could book online.

"Soph. We've a change of plans for this afternoon. Come on. We've got a van to follow."

Alex may have been a gentle, prudent sort but when something got to him he bolted forwards like a blinkered cart horse. He would do anything for his girl. Anyway, the sun had been hot and white skins were crying out for a break. Following the Ibrafly van to the launch pad sounded like a cool idea.

The drive took them on a winding road through agricultural terraces. Many had been abandoned for the more lucrative jobs of the tourist industry. But others had evidence of renewed activity born out of the first economic crisis of the 21st century and were planted with anything from corn or potatoes to vineyards.

The drive along the precipitous Tigaiga ridge was stunning. Just before turning west around a sharp bend in the road they noticed a huge statue of a naked man with his considerable manhood hanging out towards the precipice. But it was not designed to promote an interest in sexuality. The sculptor portrayed a man's desperate cry to his gods. It was Bentor, a young pre-Hispanic King believed to have plunged off the cliff towards the end of the 15th century rather than be enslaved by the Spanish conquerors.

Just a couple of hundred metres higher the paragliders had their launch pad and they too took turns to plunge off the cliff. Watching the men and women taking a short run before lifting off from their specially prepared slope was enthralling and frightening too, especially as they almost jumped into the unknown, with the sudden, thick cloud swallowing them up. Alex and Sophie decided to leave that adventure to the end of their holiday, if there was time.

It was mid-afternoon when they began to drive down from the place on the mountain ridge known as *La Corona,* the crown. But they must have missed a turn-off in the mist and when Alex realised that they had a puncture they had just passed a church in a town called *Icod el Alto.* Alex wasn't sure if he had driven that way when they followed Ibrahim's van.

"Bugger it!" cursed Alex when he finally got the spare wheel out. "This bloody tyre is flat too!"

There was not a soul to be seen in the street and the cloud was beginning to spit. Alex sat back in the car and took out the agency papers from the glove compartment. There was just a hint of a signal on his mobile phone and he dialled the number on the form, ready to give someone a touch of American hell. There was no reply. He tried again and again. Still no reply. Bloody typical!

Alex told his girlfriend, who had wrapped a beach towel around her knees, to wait in the car while he went to seek help. There was what looked like a shop on the other side of the road and the door at the top of cement steps was open. He strode over. The big sign above the door suggested the place was a hardware store owned by someone called *Hermogenes*.

Alex would have to be patient. A customer was helping the man behind the counter separate an infinite quantity of nuts and bolts. Counting them appeared to be a very slow process which required vast amounts of concentration. The age of self-service and long queues at the giant multinational stores had mercifully not yet reached this retailer in the hills of Tenerife. Whilst Alex flip-flopped and twitched in the doorway these two gentlemen fingered their nuts and bolts with deliberation, apparently oblivious to his presence.

When both men were satisfied that they had counted an exact number of nuts and bolts the man standing behind the counter, Hermogenes himself, turned his head and looked up sleepily at the American.

What happened immediately afterwards could only have come from a scene in an early black and white movie. Hermogenes leapt backwards as if he had received an electric shock from a loose cable under the old counter.

"*Dios Santo.* God Almighty!" he exclaimed, making the sign of the cross several times as if he had seen the devil and then emphasized his apparent shock with a whole line of common Spanish expletives.

The client who had been assisting Hermogenes with the counting turned around and promptly made his own use of the colourful Spanish language by uttering similar expletives to those of the storekeeper. He also crossed himself countless times while looking at Alex up and down.

Before the matter could get further out of hand, and Alex being more interested in getting the wheel fixed and Sophie safely back to La Hacienda de las Cuatro Ventanas, he pointed through the window towards the stricken car with the punctured tyre.

His explanation, with the odd word Alex thought might be Spanish, and gesticulations an orchestral conductor would have been proud of, apparently made everything perfectly clear, for an instant at least.

It was evident to the young American that the face of *el ingles,* himself in other words, had stirred an extraordinary first reaction in the two gentlemen. It might easily be described as terror. Nevertheless, known for their hospitality and generous spirit towards foreign visitors, the counting of nuts and bolts was put aside while the two men discussed what to do to help the man in the flip flops, the red and white striped swimming trunks and tutti-frutti-coloured shirt.

With a punctured tyre and a flat spare they would require a *grua* to tow the vehicle up the road to *Paco* the mechanic.

While Hermogenes made the call an old fellow with a walking stick and a little black dog entered the store. The little dog looked as if it needed a dentist to fit it out with some braces. The old man's was a huge and white-toothed smile and he greeted Alex as if he were a member of the family. In fact he appeared to refer to the colourful shorts and shirt the American wore.

"*Muchacho*, it's a bit early for carnival isn't it?"

Alex smiled back and shrugged without understanding a word.

"What *vino* have you been on this time?" insisted the old gent, obviously directing his question to Alex.

"*No es* Esteban. He is not Esteban, *hombre!*" butted in Hermogenes. He came to the foreigner's assistance after putting the telephone down.

"Can't you see he is an *extranjero*? The car of *el ingles* has a problem with a wheel. Paco is coming down with the *grua*."

The old man, whose name was Gregorio incidentally, continued to smile. But his look was a kind of empty one and suddenly he seemed to forget why he had come into the store. In fact the door was pushed open by a middle-aged woman wearing a wide straw hat with a blue ribbon.

"Every day he is worse," she apologised to Hermogenes in a gruff voice. "His bloody *memoria.*"

She was Dolores. The old fellow with the mongrel was her father. Her apologies were never needed. Everyone loved Gregorio and his afternoon visits to the store had become routine. Dolores listened to Hermogenes' brief introduction to the farce and then followed his nod towards the foreigner.

Her immediate reaction was similar, in the use of words, to those which had preceded hers.

"Coño!" she swore, grabbing old Gregorio's arm.

"Que susto, madre de dios! What a fright, mother of God!

"But he is *igualito, igualito!"* she exclaimed, tugging at her father's hand to walk him out of the store.

*"Ave María purísima....*Holy Mary, Mother of God!" she added, letting the door close behind her.

Hermogenes managed to utter a few erratic words in a dialect sometimes referred to as *Spanglish*. It was enough for Alex to understand. He appeared to have been mistaken for someone called Esteban, the grandson of Doña Isabelita, the oldest of old man Gregorio's seven sisters.

"You are like mirror. Hair is *rubio*, very blonde. Beard is ginger. You are same. You are he," explained Hermogenes.

"You wait. The *grua* is coming. Paco will fix wheel at his *taller*," Hermogenes assured Alex.

The American returned to the car to explain what was going on to Sophie. To be honest, he wasn't all together sure *what* was going on. Nor was he quite able to make her understand the bit about the blonde hair and the ginger beard and the carnival. So he was very relieved when the tow truck pulled up in front of them.

Paco hopped out to inspect. He too crossed himself religiously upon meeting Alex.

The American was opening the boot of the car to show the man that the spare tyre was also flat when he noticed a line of people following Dolores across the road and towards them. It was now drizzling quite hard out of the mist and there were a few umbrellas.

They had all come to have a look at the American who looked like Esteban dressed in touristy clothes. They were all crossing themselves and the sound of drizzle on the road was almost drowned by the whispering and the murmur in the crowd.

This was not the end of the day Alex was hoping for. In fact, strange religious fervour directed towards him and his lovely girlfriend made them both shiver and dampened their young hearts more than the drizzle.

Until some sort of an explanation made them understand.

To cut a long story short, Paco needed to tow the car to his garage. It was a short distance but gave the mechanic enough time to explain to Alex that he was the spitting image of the young man called Esteban. The man with the *grua* also made them understand that young Esteban was dead. He had suffered a motorcycle accident after a fiesta a year earlier. His body and the twisted metal of his motorcycle were discovered by chance by a farmer tending to his potato terraces deep in a mountain gully. It was close to the town of La Guancha, where Esteban had moved in to a flat. He had been getting it ready before asking his *novia* to marry him.

More people passed by the mechanic's workshop to get a peep at Alex. Others spread the news. Like all *Canarios* Alex and Sophie encountered during their few days of holiday in Tenerife, they were so kind and hospitable and curious. But the people in Icod el Alto who found themselves face to face with Alex were more than curious. They had seen a ghost.

One of the women who came to Paco's garage was Dolores. She had taken her father, Gregorio, back home and arrived at the garage just as Alex and Sophie were about to drive away. She had come to tell Alex that old Doña Isabelita wanted to meet him. There was time, of course, but the tyres had been repaired and Alex could see how uncomfortable Sophie was and decided she had already had enough emotions for one day.

"*Otro día,*" he said. "Another day. Thank you. We must go now."

Dolores seemed to understand and, as Alex started the car, she put her hand into her apron pocket. She pulled out an envelope which she handed to Alex through the car window.

□□□□□□□□□

A week's holiday for the adventurous tourist in Tenerife is just not enough. There is so much to explore on what is like a miniature continent. Almost every valley has its own micro-climate and the variety of landscapes and flora conjures up a vision of paradise long before the rabid construction industry began to entice package tourism, especially along the coast on the south of the island. Indeed it must have been paradise for the pre-Hispanic Guanche kingdoms.

Not long after their romantic holiday together Sophie decided to leave her gentle anthropologist. He was perhaps a little too much like a slow moving dinosaur although, to be fair, she had begun to feel that she was just another in his line of girlfriends.

Alex took Spanish lessons and began to investigate the origins of the Guanche people of the Canary Islands. Most theorists suggested the pre-Hispanic peoples came from the Numidian ancient Berber regions of North Africa and that they may have been brought to the islands by Phoenicians or by Romans, possibly looking for the murex mollusc, source of the famed purple dye of Tyre.

The young researcher became very excited in the early hours of one morning when he came across another well-documented idea. It asserted, albeit extravagantly, that there might have been a connection between a whiter and taller tribe of Guanche in the Canary Islands and an ancient Egyptian people. It was the sign he was looking for and any thought of discovering a replacement for Sophie was immediately put on hold. Alex launched himself into a doctorate in anthropology.

He smiled when he remembered the encounter with the islanders in Icod El Alto and decided to give his project a name. His doctorate would be called *The Guanche Kingdoms of the Canary Islands, Past and Present.*

In the spring of 2017 Alex's research took him back to the Canary Islands. This time it was going to be a prolonged stay and he rented an apartment in the university city of La Laguna. He had already exchanged correspondence with Professor Fernando Dominguez from the University of La Laguna's Department of Anthropology and Ancient History. The Professor was keen to help and introduced Alex to other members of the department. The city, which is a World Heritage Site, was also conveniently placed for the north airport from where short flights could take him to other islands. But first stop on his agenda was the Museum of Nature and Man in Santa Cruz, home to numerous Guanche mummies and other archaeological artefacts. The tram from La Laguna dropped him right in front of the magnificent building.

Second on his list of important things to do was a drive to Icod el Alto to visit Hermogenes. The envelope which Dolores had handed him through the car window a year earlier at Paco's garage had contained a photograph. Alex never showed it to Sophie but it had intrigued and worried him. He needed to find out more and hoped the old lady called Doña Isabelita would still be around to see him.

The photograph was of Esteban, the man from La Guancha, and he was indeed too like Alex for comfort. The blonde head of hair, the mischievous smile, the self-assured look in his eye, the ginger beard. That might have been the main reason why Alex had shaved off his own beard soon after returning to England with Sophie. The image of his dead double haunted him.

He decided he was going to treat this like a separate and personal investigation. He also put a name to it. In a minor and eccentric tribute to Cervantes he would call it *The Man from La Guancha.*

Hermogenes greeted Alex like a long-lost friend. By mid-day on his first Saturday back on the island of Tenerife Alex was walking up a goat track along the edge of a ravine with Dolores. He was going to see the aged Isabelita.

Young Esteban had lived with his grandmother for many years before he found the right girl. His mother and only child of Isabelita had died at the age of thirty six after a horrible struggle with cancer. Nobody, except his mother, ever knew who Esteban's father was. Esteban himself had struggled with drink and drugs and that may have been the principal cause of his motorcycle accident in the dark hours of the night.

Isabelita was now ninety years old and her skin, like a wrinkled potato from one of the terraces around her simple stone cottage, betrayed years of hard labour in the fields and in the mountain air. Nevertheless, her voice was a vigorous soprano and she possessed a ferocious look in her eyes. When they smiled, however, they were of the most beautiful blue Alex had ever seen, and Isabelita smiled a lot.

Perhaps she was descended from one of those great, white Guanche Kings.

Alex spent more than just a day with Isabelita. Alex had learnt enough Spanish for them to spend long hours in deep conversation. There was something beyond just conversation. There was an understanding and they opened up to each other. There were also more photographs.

One in particular, a slightly faded black and white photograph, showed a girl sitting against a rock on a beach. She had her arms wrapped around her knees and the smile of a fifteen year old in love. Next to her, lying on the sand with a hand propping up a handsome head was a long legged young man, probably in his early twenties. He didn't look Spanish.

"Who are they?" enquired Alex.

"*Soy yo*. It is when I was just a *niña*. The man is the father of my daughter, Amparo. *Que descanse en paz.* May they both rest in peace!

"Here, I have another one. You can keep it. I do not know why I still have it."

For a moment Isabelita hesitated as if she regretted parting with an old friend, and her eyes looked deep into Alex's as if they wanted to transmit a thought.

The photograph showed a slim, good looking young man with rolled up trousers and bare feet leaning against a pine tree. It was of the same man lying on the beach next to Isabelita when she was a young girl. Alex was never sure what made him accept the photograph but he did. He slipped it into the note book he always carried in his jacket pocket.

On his third visit to Isabelita's cottage she presented Alex with a basket full of small, black grapes from her own vines. It was late September and in Icod El Alto they were all busy with the *vendimia,* the grape harvest.

Isabelita also produced a jug with cool red wine. It was her own wine and surprisingly good. After an initial note of sulphur, he discovered an earthy taste of mulberry in the wine and it soon swallowed very easily. Old Isabelita was quite a connoisseur.

"We like to drink this wine when it is young and cool, a bit like myself," she laughed after another tiny glass followed the first.

The cool brew made them both laugh and they shared a board with fresh goat cheese and dried figs. Glass of wine after another mellowed the old lady and her thoughts and memories began to flow.

"I think I loved him. I hope I did!" she added with a twinkle of her blue eye.

When Isabelita was a young girl she had been sent down to the Orotava Valley to learn the art of drawn-thread embroidery under the employment of a wealthy British merchant. Spain's bitter civil war had been followed immediately by the Second World War and times were extremely difficult. Local families found it hard to feed their flock.

It was 1942. Whilst thousands found it easier to risk their lives emigrating across the Atlantic in search of a future, others couldn't. Any offer of a safe job on the island was better for a young girl than labouring on the mountain terraces.

In the Orotava Valley Isabelita was given a bed, food and a small salary. In return she would help with the household chores and be instructed in sewing and embroidery. She was also able to have Sundays free to herself, although it goes without saying that she was expected to accompany other employees to church. Everyone went to church.

One of the regular prayers offered by the priest in Puerto de la Cruz was for God to help General Franco maintain Spain as a neutral state whilst Germany went about her business. News had filtered through, even to the poorer classes. The Spanish dictator and victor of the civil war had met Adolf Hitler. They had discussed Germany's plans for capturing Gibraltar in order to control the Mediterranean.

Trade between the islands and the rest of the world had already been seriously disrupted and any contact between the British Isles and the Canary Islands had virtually ceased as

German U Boats hunted down any allied shipping steaming up and down the African coast and into the Atlantic. Many ships were sunk within or not far from Canary Island waters.

British convoy SL-125, bound for Manchester from Suez via Durban and Freetown had made steady progress without incident until its ships sailed past the islands on 28th October, 1942.

At just after 22.00 hours German Submarine U-509, captained by Werner Witte, fired five torpedoes towards the convoy. Two of the torpedoes hit random targets. A vessel called the Hopecastle was damaged and later finished off by another German submarine. There were no survivors. The other ship hit was the Nagpore. She was owned by the P&O Steam Navigation Company. She was carrying 7,000 tons of general cargo including 1,500 tons of copper. Twenty members of her crew, including the ship's master, lost their lives. Twenty three survivors were picked up by Frigate HMS Crocus. Eighteen others spent fourteen days adrift in a lifeboat before being towed ashore by a *falua* from the port of Puerto de la Cruz on the coast of the Orotava Valley.

The seamen were in a very poor state, severely dehydrated and fried by the sun and salt. But they had survived. A neutral ship would be found which would take them to another safe haven or to a neutral state. A Spanish ship bound for Central America eventually took them via Brazil to Panama. From there they found their way to the U.S.A. before returning home to England. While they waited for a safe passage the merchant sailors spent some weeks in the Orotava Valley. Most were dispersed amongst compassionate Spanish families who fed them up and treated them like welcome angels. Two or three were handed over to the British Vice-Consulate in Puerto de la Cruz and consequently placed with British residents whose own young men were doing their duty somewhere.

One of these was the twenty one year old man in the photograph which Isabelita had given to Alex Marriot. All she knew was that he was called Giles, although she found the name difficult to pronounce. He became the guest of the family she worked and sewed for. He was given a room in the main house although he took his meals in the kitchen with the other employees.

Giles recovered quickly from his ordeal and was keen to help in any way he could to pay for his keep. In a very short time he was helping the men load bunches of bananas onto the family's lorry and running errands. He even learnt to skin rabbits and to milk the cows.

The first time he noticed Isabelita she was in the kitchen with other maids. They were having their morning *desayuno*, a bowl of coffee and milk as well as balls of *gofio* with mashed bananas, sugar and lemon juice. She glanced at him briefly as he entered through the swing door carrying two containers filled with fresh, warm milk from the cow shed. When his eyes met her deep blue jewels she quickly looked down as if she had been caught out doing something forbidden.

Isabelita did feel she had done something forbidden because she had heard the other girls talking about the handsome seaman, his sun-bleached blonde curls and his slim, muscular body.

The next time Giles and Isabelita made eye contact was when he was running down the main staircase into the courtyard. She was closing the door to the sewing room which was in the servants' quarters and led off from the courtyard. God had evidently told her she was not forbidden to make contact with the handsome man and on this occasion she was entirely self-assured. Possibly too much.

"Buenos días ingles!" she greeted, teasing him with a smile before pulling the door closed behind her.

Similar brief encounters occurred over the next days and furtive glances across the church aisle and over the pews the following Sunday confirmed mutual interest.

Alex listened intently to Isabelita's story.

"People said I was just an innocent child and I suppose I should have been," Isabelita sighed.

"But I regret that I wasn't. I try to excuse myself by being sure that I really was in love. He was so *guapo* and strong and at the same time tender with me. But, *ay señor,* I played with fire just as my daughter Amparo did with her man.

"I teased and enticed the beautiful Giles," confessed Isabelita. Indeed she had done. The young English seaman was enticed and he understood no bounds.

"We spoke a different language but our eyes understood and our bodies responded."

The first time it happened was in the shallows of a rock pool next to a beach known as *El Bollullo.* In those distant days it had not yet become the popular bay it is today and it was a long way to walk through the banana plantations, across a ravine and down the cliff on a track used by fishermen. The expedition was arranged by the men and women who worked for Isabelita's British employers. They often had outings to the seaside or into the hills.

The picnic of potatoes, salted fish, fruit, *gofio*, cheeses and wine led to playful games on the black, volcanic sand and before long they all collapsed under makeshift canopies of strung-up sheets and palm leaves.

There was another family gathering on the beach. One of its members was a young man called Imeldo Baeza, the grandson of one of the island's finest artists. Imeldo was never without a camera and he became one of Tenerife's best known photographers. He entertained himself and everyone else on the beach with a series of photographic sessions. It was he who took the photograph which Isabelita had shown Alex of her and Giles on the beach.

It was quite soon after that photograph was taken, when the humid air, the cups of wine and the lapping waves rocked people into a siesta that Giles and Isabelita took their stroll. They climbed over a mound of rocks towards the west of the El Bollullo beach, occasionally looking behind them to make sure they were not followed. Just beyond the rocks they discovered the private sanctuary of their rock pool.

It was inevitable and natural. The swell of the tide brought waves of fresh, frothing water into the pool and over their nakedness and Isabelita entwined her legs around him.

The English seaman and the Canary Island apprentice were secret lovers frequently, mostly on the uncomfortable bed of pine needles that carpeted the cow shed. Once, on another excursion to the pine forests of Aguamansa, they were almost found out.

Then, suddenly one day, just five weeks after Giles and Isabelita had become lovers it all came to a rushing end. It was crack of dawn when a small military-looking lorry came up the drive through the bananas. Giles recognised some of his fellow seamen sitting in rows at the back. He was told to grab his belongings and left without a thank you or a goodbye to his hosts. Nor was there time or a thought perhaps for a whisper to his fifteen year old lover. A working voyage had been arranged for Giles and the rest of his mates on a ship bound for Brazil.

When her pregnancy was discovered Isabelita was sent back to her family in the hills. Giles was never heard of again by anyone on the island.

A hint of tear in old Isabelita's eyes told Alex Marriot that it was time to return to his other anthropological investigations in La Laguna.

□□□□□□□□□□

A month after returning to Cambridge Alex received news from America that his mother, Joyce, had passed away unexpectedly. He was given time off from his field studies for the university and flew to the States in time for her funeral. He was surprised to see his father, Jim, amongst the mourners. His parents' divorce had been so sullied with bitter recriminations. Somehow their encounter did give father and son a chance to make some kind of peace.

Jim Marriot also told his son that after he, Alex, decided to make his life in England he and his mother had made efforts to forgive each other. Jim also told Alex that it had been his mother's wish that he should have her house in San Diego, California. It wasn't much of a place but it was his if he wanted it and any possessions he wished to keep. Almost ceremoniously Jim Marriot handed the house keys over to Alex in front of his mother's grave.

Alex Marriot's mother, after the divorce in 2011, had gone back to using her maiden name. That is why the name on the wooden post box at the bottom of the front garden was Joyce Agnew.

The house had little of interest inside, just a few cheap paintings, quite a nice old gramophone which Alex decided to keep and some rather ageing furniture. His mother seemed to have led a solitary life and unfortunately there was evidence of drinking.

Empty bottles of bourbon had found space in different cupboards. It saddened Alex.

There were some old books and magazines on the shelf above the drinks cabinet and they were propped up at one end by what looked like a much heavier ledger. Out of curiosity Alex pulled it down and almost choked on the dust.

To his surprise and pleasure it was a tatty, old leather-bound photograph album. The faded ink letters on the leather binding told him it was the wedding day photograph album of Giles and Ernestine Agnew. When he turned the first page he couldn't believe his eyes.

There was Giles, the same good looking young man with rolled up trousers and bare feet leaning against a pine tree in the photograph which Isabelita had given him. This time he wore a swanky, ivory tuxedo. His full name was Giles Hamish Agnew and he had gone to live in the Unites States after the war. There he was with Alex's grandmother, Ernestine Zenker on their wedding day!

Alex Marriot sat back and closed his eyes as the story began to sink in and make sense. Giles, the English merchant seaman, the lover of fifteen year old Isabelita in a Canary Island rock pool was Giles Agnew, his maternal grandfather. He, Alex the anthropologist and Esteban, the man from La Guancha, would have been half-cousins.

A SHARK IN THE BATH

My darling mother was enjoying the beach, sitting on her rickety deck chair and reading through a Marguerite Patten recipe book. I have no doubt she was conjuring up a surprise for one of her frequent dinner parties.

My father had taken on more diplomatic duties from his ailing brother, who was British Vice-Consul in Puerto de la Cruz. Life was one big party. Actually, Father was not a party man and much preferred the freedom of the local, uninhibited ways and often did his best to escape to the barren lands of the south of Tenerife. His excuse was to do business with the tomato farmers. But my mother was an entertainer by nature and considered giving dinner parties an important part of her duties as a member of one of the Canary Island's oldest British families.

Father had departed from our hotel at the crack of dawn to drive the old Land Rover as far as the hillside town of Arafo. He was going to see his friend, Eduardo Curbelo, a southern landowner who grew vines, tomatoes and onions. After returning from Africa in the late 1940s he began to buy Curbelo's and other growers' tomatoes for a Glasgow fruit merchant called Ian Mcleod. Dad would join us later for a picnic lunch on the beach when he had finished visiting the tomato terraces. With any luck he would get Cipriano, the fisherman, to take us out in his boat in the early evening.

Business and pleasure went hand in hand. Tenerife in the 1960s was still a sleepy island with an unhurried pattern to life and my father had decided to bring us along on his rounds. This meant missing school for two or three days and getting up to innocent mischief on the beach.

Mummy could easily have been mistaken for a famous American actress such was her elegant posture beside the gently rising tide. In fact her exterior demeanour hid a quiet simplicity. This often clashed with her love for a colourful party and she was the kindest and most generous person I have ever met. She was always most gracious and almost innocent, I sometimes believed, in acknowledging comments of admiration from passing gentlemen.

She had been catching the morning sun under a wide, straw hat which she always adorned with glorious silk scarves to match her swimsuit or beach towel. Her beautiful skin was discovering a more sensual, olive tone and her turquoise eyes shone even more than the glistening sea.

So I should perhaps have been more understanding of those Latin spectators. I think I may have been quite rude to them when my mother pretended not to notice. I suppose it was my way of defending her, or perhaps of defending what was mine.

I soon plunged back into the sea and forgot all about what was mine. Anyway, my mother had descended deep into animated conversation with a family from Santa Cruz and was safe.

The Spanish family were also staying for two or three days at the El Médano Hotel. It had been the first proper hotel on the south coast of Tenerife, the side of the island which would in a few years' time become a vast tourist empire.

But this was 1964 and the hotel was only a year old. With a new road reaching most of the south coast of Tenerife it quickly became the in-place for affluent inhabitants of Santa Cruz and northern towns of Tenerife to escape for a few days. It was erected on what was originally the site of an old tomato packing shed. Indeed the tiny fishing port at El Médano had grown as a result of transporting tomatoes to other parts of the island by sea long before roads became more than dusty tracks.

Our neighbours on the vast stretch of sand had settled down only feet away from us. This is a natural phenomenon. It is standard procedure on beaches where the culture is to be sociable and noisy as opposed to reserved and intolerant. One would easily think they must have been scared of great open spaces. But the custom, as irritating as it might sometimes be to the newly arrived northerner, reflects a spirit we could do well not to scorn. It is a sign of generosity and friendship.

This school of city-dwellers next to us on the beach were an elderly gentleman with a walking stick and a grey fedora covering a balding head, three grand *señoras* and a skinny young girl. The ladies, all of whom were extremely un-beach-worthy (in other words rather plump) sat fully clothed under a makeshift tent. This consisted of a bed sheet hung up with string, clothes pegs and wooden poles. While the old gentleman leaned on his stick and buried his toes in the sand the ladies knitted, painted finger nails and took turns to remark about anybody else who caught their imagination.

One moment they appeared outraged by the *sinverguenzas*, those insolent scoundrels who passed by and molested the foreign *señora*. The next, with a sharp swing of their necks, they turned their attention to a young Scandinavian lady who now became the target for those hungry male eyes. She was showing even more of a body than my mother and certainly more than they were accustomed to. There was little else to do on a beach.

Accompanying the ladies was a grandchild. She was what my mother referred to as a sweet little girl of my age but whom I was refusing to consider as an alternative source of interest. She may have been a reason for my hiding in the sea for so long.

Carmen, our maid servant, with whom I shared a room at the hotel, had just struggled to bring herself across the sand with the picnic basket. My mother called out, pointed at our bucket and asked me to fill it with seawater. It was to keep my father's beer cool. It was quite a large and heavy recipient made of zinc and had once been used for milking the family's two cows. *Flaca* and *Pepita* had been sold to a neighbour so the bucket now had other uses. It was also handy when boys like me went hunting for innocent crabs and gullible blennies in the rock pools.

The sea, early in November, was quite cool after the first of the season's rains had swept down from the north Atlantic a few days earlier. Mount Teide also sparkled in his first winter coat. But the wind, which so often adds sand to the ingredients of a picnic and makes El Médano such a paradise for windsurfers today, was keeping offshore.

It was blissful for a seven year old like me. All I needed now was for Emilio, a local friend I had made the day before, to finish his morning classes. I was eager to continue with the innocent explorations of the shallows which had kept us so very busy soon after breakfast. While my mother had been enjoying her breakfast with a coffee on the hotel's terrace, a kind of pier on wooden stilts over the sea, he and I had begun to invent mischief.

When I returned with the bucket and to lie beside my mother it was still only mid-morning but the yellow sand under my body was already deliciously warm in spite of the thinning, high cloud. So I used my arms, like a tortoise, to enclose my sides with the fine El Médano grain.

I felt Carmen cover my back and shoulders with a towel. Like most Canary Islanders she was thoughtful and grateful. She was also a friend and almost a part of the family. Before very long my eyes closed and I lost myself in what I imagine must have been a daydream.

I was Lawrence of Arabia. He was my childhood hero. My father had taken me to see David Lean's magnificent film about the life of T.E. Lawrence and his adventures on the Arabian Peninsula. The Englishman's eccentric heroism made a profound impression on me.

My left cheek nestled on the warm sand and the beach was my desert in the Hejaz regions of Arabia. I was listening out for the sound of a distant train which was transporting Turkish guns and ammunition. On the horizon, beyond the sands towards Medina, the El Médano Hotel may have been the Sarawat Mountains. The lapping of the waves was quite like the padding hooves of a camel approaching from afar. It was a mirage playing tricks with my dream. Or perhaps it was not.

My half closed eyes focused on the advancing enemy. What they saw in the haze was not Omar Sharif, as Sherif Ali approaching on the camel, but a gangling figure making haste towards us across the sand. He was a tall, thin man and he wore a dark suit. The gentleman had a long stride and his left arm swung out erratically as if it were an uncontrolled supplement used to balance a furious internal discussion. I seem to remember he was talking to himself or rehearsing a speech.

The man with the long stride and the erratic arm was the hotel manager, Don Faustino. He was not a beach person and his pointed nose, tiny grey eyes and pale face gave him a deathly appearance.

He came to a halt, as did the mirage in my imagination, and offered my mother a polite but strained, *buenos días, señora.*

"*Buenos días*," she replied cheerfully over her pretty, winged sunglasses.

"There is a shark in the bath!" exclaimed Faustino in a rather high-pitched, desperate-sounding voice. That was obviously the sentence he had been rehearsing as he approached our patch on the beach.

I can't begin to imagine what the poor man must have felt at my mother's reaction. I am certain he was expecting an immediate state of shock, overwhelming apologies or even understanding.

Instead my darling mother began to laugh a most joyous, hearty laugh. The last time I heard her laugh in that fashion was when she took me to see an amateur production of Arsenic and Old Lace at the British Games Club in Puerto de la Cruz. I suppose it was the absurdity of the man's announcement that started her off.

Looking back at the scene, I have to accept her initial reaction. For an instant I really believed she thought poor Faustino possessed a sense of humour. A shark in a bath? How ludicrous!

Naturally, in the manager's mind, there was nothing in the least bit funny. He might easily have turned his back on my mother in disgust and walked away. How could such a serious situation not have the English lady begging with apologies in absolute horror?

Don Faustino didn't surrender, of course. Instead he turned his attention to the horrible little boy, to me.

Like an eel I slithered back into the sea. There was nothing heroic, like Lawrence of Arabia, in my retreat. Mine was a sudden realisation that I was in deep water, in a whole lot of trouble. I'm afraid to admit that I did something my father always said I should never do. I turned my back on the enemy.

There was worse to come. The old grey Land Rover came to a halt in a swirl of dust above the beach. It was my father and he was not alone. With him as passengers were two Guardia Civil police officers. I saw them vigorously dust down their olive-green uniforms. When my father pointed in our direction they straightened their extraordinary tri-corn hats and appeared to look directly at me. I had no doubt at all. I was going to be arrested.

I was shivering. I can't remember if it was the cold water or the fear. However I decided to leave the safety of my shelter, the sea, and wrapped myself in the warm dune again, this time at a safe distance from our party. I spied, like a Bedouin tribesman, over the mound of sand my arms quickly created into a protective barricade.

I remember events unfolding at a relentless pace, especially for one facing punishment.

I sensed a flicker of hope, however. The Guardia Civil officers saluted my father and disappeared into *Casa Pepe*, the bar on the *plaza*.

Father marched down towards our beach camp with a huge smile for my mother. She waved and Faustino looked towards her husband with an expression of relief. At least here was someone who would listen.

"Hello darling! Ah, Don Faustino, *Buenos días!*" greeted my father, undoing his tie and targeting the sea for a splash.

Walking through the tomato plantations, talking to the workers and testing the quality of the produce was always a favourite pastime but he invariably returned coated in dust or mud, depending on the season.

"*Buenos días* Don Noel!" echoed the manager nervously.

"I am very, very sorry Sir, but there is a very big, big problem!"

"Yes, I'm hot and I need a swim and a

beer!" replied my father cheerfully. For someone who had fought and been injured several times in world war battles any problem could wait and be answered with a smile.

But he politely waited for the problem and searched inside Faustino's anxious eyes.

"There is a shark in the bath!" repeated the manager with a sudden, jerky swing of his left arm.

"*Qué*?" replied my father, looking sideways at my mother for some kind of complicity.

"In the bathroom, Sir. There is a shark in the bath!"

"Oh, don't be ridiculous! What on Earth are you talking about, man?"

I seem to remember my father looking very impatient. Then, after deciding to study Don Faustino's face more closely he must have come to the natural conclusion.

"Where is John?" he growled, looking all about until he spotted a familiar yellow head disguised behind the sand bunker.

"Come here!"

The tone required immediate attention and within seconds I was standing slightly behind my darling mother.

Instinctively I expected her motherly protection. But she was not that kind of darling mother. Having been brought up with three brothers in the African bush she expected her offspring to fend for themselves at a very young age.

It was evident that the hotel manager, in spite of his black-suited menace and sharp nose pointed directly at me, showed a nervous, hyena-like respect for my father. I still have visions of Don Faustino circling at a safe distance for my father to finish with me.

Then, when he thought the more powerful beast had had his share, the hotel manager's plaintive explanation opened the proceedings. It was like a courtroom on a beach, my father acting as the presiding judge.

It was in Room 66 where it all happened.

Apparently, the new room attendant, Inmaculada, a young girl from the hillside town of Arico, had gone in to clean the bathroom in Room 66. It was a room facing the hills which I was sharing with Carmen. It was just before eleven o'clock.

Inmaculada, who had never even smelt sea air before coming to work at El Médano Hotel, had been told to clean the bathrooms before making the beds. In all other bathrooms which she had cleaned that morning there was the usual evidence of a shower having been used and, in a few, sand from the beach carelessly introduced by human feet. The fine sand on this particular beach had a habit of travelling on feet, towels, sandwiches and anything else that had been taken to the water's edge. In Room 66 there was not only sand. The white hotel towels had been carefully placed on the floor around the bath. The bath, she had reported, was brimming full.

What had made Inmaculada run screeching out of Room 66 was the sight of something long and grey-brown lying motionless at the bottom of the bath. In her state of near hysteria the girl didn't consider a closer inspection to discover what it might be. What she was absolutely certain about was that it was not a toy, rubber fish.

It was a shark. There was a shark in the bath. A dead shark. It may have been alive two hours earlier but, like most creatures of its kind it would be intolerant to fresh water. It would need to move constantly to provide a supply of oxygenated sea water in order to survive. Unlike normal fish, it would not turn upside down and float. It would sink, upright, to the bottom.

It was a young hound shark. Fishermen in the Canary Islands call it a *cazón*. An adult can be as long as fifty five inches. The poor specimen in Room 66 measured just thirty five inches, including its long, heterocercal caudal fin. But it was still a shark! This species can be found marauding sandy depths in packs and usually well below thirty feet. The shark in the bath may have been disorientated and became lost in the shallows. It may have been injured in some way, perhaps by a fisherman's net.

However unusual it was to find a shark like this in the shallow waters of a beach this one had found its way into my hands. I had been exploring the rock pools and sandbanks with my new friend, Emilio. We were splashing about chasing a shoal of young golden grey mullet when Emilio shouted.

"Coñoooo. Corre, sal del agua!"

The first word was an extended version of a rather vulgar term used in Spanish speaking countries for a woman's sexual anatomy. However, due to its common use as an expletive it is considered almost an essential part of the Spanish language, even in the noblest of circles. The second part of his warning was telling me to get the hell out of the water.

It was too late. The *cazón* was upon me and I felt and saw it passing between my legs. It was not chasing the mullet. Nor did it take a sample of my flesh. I knew instinctively that it was in trouble and when a very gentle wave rolled the creature on its side, I realised that this shark needed help.

Without thinking I placed my hands under the shark as if I were tickling a trout in a Highland burn and lifted it gently out of the sea.

"Vamos, come on," I shouted at Emilio as I ran to pick up my towel.

"Muchacho, what are you going to do?" he

asked as he caught me up.

"Here, wet the towel. I'm going to take it home," I replied urgently.

"*Hombre. Estás como una cabra!*" Emilio insisted, telling me that I was behaving like a goat. In other words, in Canary Island terms, he thought I was off my rocker.

But Emilio didn't understand. If he had been brave enough to catch it he would undoubtedly have taken the creature home for his mother to cook. El Médano was a seaside village. Anything caught swimming in the sea ended up in a pot. I, on the other hand, was being brought up on the Encyclopaedia Britannica and Gerald Durrell. Therefore, if I hadn't hooked it and it was injured, like a bird with a broken wing, I had to help it. Of course it would also look splendid in the garden pond. In the excitement of the early morning hunt, it simply didn't occur to me that fresh water was only for fresh water fish.

But, like a brilliant strategist, the boy of action had it all worked out in a flash. The wet towel had two objectives. The first was to keep the shark moist. The other was to sneak it into the hotel, into the modern lift into which I was forbidden from entering without an adult, and into Room 66.

The mission completed, having filled the bath with cold water, Emilio and I returned to our placid hunting grounds of the Médano shore until a shout and a whistle summoned my friend to his school lessons. Until the appearance of the hotel manager on the beach, I forgot all about our shark in the bath.

I remember that we had been invited, on that same evening of my shark adventure, to dine at the Curbelo's house in Arafo. It became a late Friday night but Dad kept his promise. He always did. The next day we went out fishing with Cipriano in his boat. Thus my adventures on the beach with my friend Emilio were soon lost in memory and exhaustion.

The following day was Sunday and we would be departing for home. So, with promises that I could go and play one last time with Emilio early in the morning, I, like any good little boy in the 1960s, was bathed, supped and put to bed soon after sunset.

Knowing that Carmen would keep me out of further mischief in Room 66, my darling mother and father dressed for dinner and went to join other guests on the hotel's pier terrace. It was most elegant and my mother was feeling very romantic and daringly exotic. The sky still glowed with a glorious, after-sunset orange and waiters flurried to and fro eager to please and with trays of aperitifs.

My father, who was looking quite dashing according to my mother, asked for the chef's recommendation after they had been shown to their table.

"*Tollos señor.* Caught locally and served with wrinkled potatoes," was the head waiter's whispered proposal.

"Excellent! Please bring us some Mateus Rosé," replied my father as waves began to let their crests flirt with the moonlight.

Tollos, which is an acquired taste, was one of his favourite treats. My mother, who was never particularly fond of acquiring tastes, ordered sole meunière. Like many a local fish recipe, my father's *tollos* would have been prepared in cuts, salted and dried in the sun for a day or two. The cuts would then have been marinated for hours and gently stewed with garlic, onions, peppers and tomatoes. The local delicacy can sometimes be found on restaurant menus when they have a dish of hound shark available.

Of course, it wasn't *my* shark in the bath. There would not have been time to prepare it. Nevertheless Father was not foolish enough to provide this information to my darling mother.

If he had, any promise of romance and exotic daring that evening would have been lost at sea.

TWO WITCHES AND A FORTUNE

The air, if there was any, was still. The leaves on the banana trees at the back of the garden hung motionless. The birds had turned unnaturally silent. The dog lay on the wooden corridor floor and panted. His master's young wife, Rose, stretched out on the verandah rocking chair.

Rose loved hot, Tenerife days. They were one of the reasons she was so happy living just outside Puerto de la Cruz in the Orotava valley. But the heat in May 1952 was oppressing. It came up from the south and was caused by a storm further down the African coast. It was humid and unusually tropical. Rose felt listless and wondered if she would ever have the energy to move again. And so she remained for most of the day, sipping icy passion-fruit juice from time to time.

Suddenly the dog lifted an ear as the echo of footsteps on the floorboards revealed Encarnacion's progress. Incarnation, whom they called *Encarna* for short, was at the same time the cleaner, cook and adviser on local affairs.

"*Señora*, there are two old women at the back gate. They ask to see you. They come long way, *señora*. They walk from Santa Úrsula. They are *locas*," advised Encarna.

"I'm sure they are not mad, Encarna. But they must be thirsty and hungry."

"No. Perhaps not mad, *señora*. But in this *calor*. And they look like witches!"

"I will come along in a minute, Encarna. Please make some *parchita* juice for the ladies."

"*Si señora.*"

Incarnation had become accustomed to her young English mistress being hospitable to all sorts of strangers and her feet echoed down the corridor again. It was going to be another of those days, she thought resignedly. And this pair did look like *brujas*.

They weren't witches, of course, and Rose was quite used to Encarna calling anyone she didn't like a witch. But they could easily have passed for two of Shakespeare's Wayward Witches. The two women standing on the patio outside the kitchen were old, wrinkled, barefoot and dirty. They smelt a thousand years old.

When they saw the English rose they smiled toothless smiles and came forward and presented the *señora* with two plaits of garlic. It was their offering and, for an instant, Rose felt her Christian common sense crumble. What if they are witches, she thought.

The two women were sisters and lived near the town of Santa Ursula. They had been told of the *señora* and her kindness. They wanted to ask a favour.

There were two wooden benches under the papaya trees in the corner of the kitchen garden and Rose led them there and invited them to sit down. It was far enough away from Encarna and, anyway, she couldn't have their smell in the house, not even in the servant's quarters.

Favours normally implied giving poor people a basket of food, handing over old shoes or unused shirts and trousers or getting the neighbouring doctor to attend to an evident illness. Doctor Isidoro Luz was also the Mayor in Puerto de la Cruz but he always had time for treating the infirm and the poor. Sometimes a favour might mean lending some *pesetas* which would never be seen again. This request, however, was out of the ordinary.

"*Señora*, you are English, *no*?" began one of the sisters.

"Yes."

"There is a Bank in *Inglaterra* with a lot of

money!" butted in the second sister, getting to the point quite enthusiastically.

"It belongs to us!"

The wrinkled old lips took it in turns to explain whilst Rose listened. She didn't stop the tale because she was speechless.

"Our mother, may she rest in peace, told us before she died about the brother of her mother. He was a priest in Brazil. He owned a million pesetas. He is dead. That money he left to my mother. The money is in a bank in England."

Rose definitely gave them the impression that she didn't have a clue where this was all leading to, the favour in other words.

"You go and get our money, *señora*. You keep half."

It must be the heat. Surely, it must be the oppressive heat, thought Rose and she could only reply with a disbelieving smile.

"*Señora*. Listen to us. He was a priest with great possessions. Lands, fishing boats, gold and silver. Now all is money in a bank in England. My sister and I should inherit money."

The story just didn't find space in Rose's imagination. It was like a peculiar dream. There she was talking with two old women in rags, images of poverty in the extreme, and they spoke of such wealth like legal advisers. The extravagance of the dream was surely induced by the suffocating African air. Rose would have to put an end to their illusion. It was not the kind of favour she could grant.

"I am so sorry. You should not have come to me about this. I cannot help you."

"You want more than half? We will give you more. But you get money for these two poor *viejas*."

"No," Rose protested. "I can't help you. I am not going to England. You should go and see your priest or perhaps a lawyer. You can show him your papers. Do you want to speak to a lawyer? I know a lawyer," Rose said hopefully. Naturally, there were no papers.

The two old women departed without their favour but not before being fed a bowl of soup thickened with *gofio*. A cool breath of air accompanied them down the drive. Rose felt relieved. The oppressive heat suddenly disappeared. Even the dog stopped panting. Were they witches?

Rose thought that at last she could catch up on some letters and took a pen and paper to the table under the garden pergola.

It just wasn't to be. The old women's story

had not ended with their departure. In fact it returned when Encarna entered the scene again with the tea tray for her *señora*.

"If I may humbly say so *señora*, you were right not to help those *brujas*." The maid was still insisting in calling them witches.

"Poor old things!"

"They are greedy witches. They are jealous of each other and of everyone. They have money under their *colchón*. They just pretend," insisted Encarna.

"Of course they don't have money under their mattress, Encarna. Don't be bad. Didn't you see their clothes and their feet? I will not have you say bad things. Now will you please go down to Maximino's and ask him to bring us some red onions, potatoes and fruit."

In normal circumstance Encarna would obey the order immediately. She liked going to Maximino's. He was full of gossip. Instead, Encarna appeared to be in a trance and returned to the subject of the English bank. The African air returned.

"The money in England is ours!" she exclaimed suddenly.

"What?"

"My mother is directly descended from that priest in Brazil!"

□□□□□□□□□

It was on that sticky day in May that Rose first heard the intriguing story about the priest and his fortune. But it was not the last and the story grew and grew as spring turned to summer and the heat intensified. He was known as Father Placido and soon became the talk of the town. Even the local newspaper couldn't resist stirring up an article saturated with far-reaching implications and rumour-enticing ideas. The money was hidden under floor-boards in a London mansion. How had the priest really made such a fortune? How could a Catholic priest, sworn to celibacy, have so many descendants?

Encarna and the two witches were not the only claimants to the fortune. Legal advisers, banks and churches received visits from hopeful inheritors. So did the sympathetic English lady called Rose. They came in all shapes and sizes, from young women with calculating eyes and dangling ear-rings, to men from the banana plantations in stained whites and *lonas* on their feet.

In the end, it all came down to papers. Nobody had any papers to prove their claims and there were so many claims that no legal adviser could possibly be bothered to make the effort unless he was certain of receiving a vast bonus himself. One or two claims arrived from as far as Mexico and Spanish Guinea where it was believed Father Placido was buried.

The long hot summer came to an end and the September sea breeze cleansed the air. With it, the stories and claims about the priest's fortune seemed to blow away.

□□□□□□□□□

The same breeze at dawn made the bedroom curtains dance like Russian Ballerinas. Sandy smiled lovingly. How lucky he was to have a beautiful English rose for a wife.

Small and pale rounded breasts moved up and down and a nipple peeped at him enticingly from under her silk nightie. One day soon, he knew, they would fill for their first child. Rose had perfumed the bath with petals from the garden and bubbles and they shared the bottle of Dom Pérignon he had brought home to celebrate their anniversary. It had been a playful night and he felt himself stir once again. So did Rose as he grew against her buttock. Early morning was her favourite time for love. His body was tender and her desire and thoughts yielded to his aroma. It was not the eager love of the dark night but the prolonged and sensual love-making of two young people exploring boundaries as the curtains toyed with the light of day.

The smell of toast and coffee drifted up the staircase and breakfast was a call for different action.

"It's a good day to go and explore. I've been thinking of going to Granadilla. Would you like to come, my love?"

It meant freedom. Freedom from the house. Freedom from the boredom which so often accompanied young wives in a foreign country. Freedom from Encarna. Of course Rose would like to go!

"I'm going to see someone about water tomorrow. So there will be quite a lot of hanging around. But we'll spend the night under the stars somewhere in the hills."

"Wonderful, darling! I'll get a picnic together."

Rose was excited like a little child and in love, spilling over with love.

By late afternoon the Land Rover was speeding through the Ucanca plain at the base of Mount Teide. The fantastic Martian landscapes in what islanders call *Las Cañadas* is like another planet, so different from the lush, green lowlands of the Orotava valley. To their right as they drove into the desert-like sedimentary plain where great heaps of ancient lava flows once threatened to bury all evidence of a caldera, was the great volcano. Teide, like all around him, looked thirsty for snow.

Great crags, cliffs, strata, rocks and phonolytic dykes make this a geologist's paradise. The orange glow of the sun at the end of the day convert the tones of blacks, browns, yellows, turquoise, reds and bronze in the landscape into an even more fascinating and artistic territory. Time has not yet made this land fertile and petrified rivers of cold, purple lava look as if they flowed yesterday. Yet, there is abundant life in ponderous beetles, sunbathing lizards, skinny rabbits, unique specie of bee, the shy shrikes and the odd kestrel. It might have been the altitude playing games with the mind but the desolate landscape made Rose feel that there really was a God looking down, or a Devil tempting fate deep inside these craters.

There was certainly something satanic about the black material which spewed out during the last eruption from the *Pico Viejo* in 1798 and suddenly it was almost a relief to leave behind them the deserts and volcanic plains.

Sandy took the road to *Vilaflor* and they began to look out for their turn-off at the top of the southern pine forests. It was their usual campsite on a small balcony of ground overlooking the precipice of a deep gorge below. It was well hidden from the road and far enough to be entirely private. The Land Rover had no trouble finding its way, zigzagging through the boulders and bushes of retama and flixweed and came to a halt under the shade of three or four fat pines. A flat, basaltic rock made a perfect dining table and the stones they used as chairs had not been moved since the last time they camped here.

Rose began taking no end of things out of the picnic basket while Sandy prepared their bed inside a low wall of stones they had used to protect them from the wind on other occasions. The bed consisted of a mattress of raked up pine needles covered by a thick, canvass sheet. It had once been part of his old army tent. The purple pillows were cushions borrowed from the garden hammock and a selection of faithful, tartan rugs to hide under made for a very snug camp.

By far the best part of their camp under the pines high up in the southern hills was sometimes the clearest view of the islands of La Gomera, La Palma and El Hierro way off on the horizon. Their green mountains peeped through a sea of cloud below like ghost ships. The orange glow of the sinking sun created a constantly changing painting in the mountains and crags behind them. The sun decided to nestle between the two breasts of La Palma. It was as hypnotic as a crackling fireplace in an

English country cottage and the thin air and a cup or two of cool Chio wine conjured up another tempting, romantic evening. However, a feminine dislike of spiders and beetles persuaded Rose not to remove her jodhpurs and Sandy's nakedness under the moon became an opportunity lost.

ᴅᴅᴅᴅᴅᴅᴅᴅᴅᴅ

By nine o'clock the next morning Sandy had parked the Land Rover in a cobbled lane on the outskirts of Granadilla of Abona, one of the principal towns on the southern slopes of Tenerife. The Guanche Kingdom of Abona was one of the last to be submitted to Spanish rule and began to be inhabited by the all-conquering Spaniards in 1503. As soon as the Land Rover's purring engine stopped, shutters in the windows along the entire lane began to open and heads popped out interesting themselves in the novelty.

Sandy strode down the lane with two men. They were off to see a water gallery in which Sandy was interested in purchasing shares. There are over a thousand water galleries, or tunnels cut into the mountains of Tenerife. They were dug in search of water which seeps through the porous soil after heavy winter snows and they are owned by shareholders. There was a constant and growing demand for water and therefore for the ownership of a share or two.

Sandy did warn Rose. Her accompanying him to Granadilla would mean a lot of waiting around.

Nevertheless, the scenery was like opening a quaint book. Those heads kept popping in and out of green, brown and blue shutters, lizards peeped out through holes in the stone walls, a couple of ominous-looking raven flew past into the almond trees above the town and men, women and children began to go about their daily business. The women all seemed to hurry. The men's pace was more languid. Rose had noticed that about most men on the island. They went about their motions slowly as if they feared the sun would drain all their energy if they walked faster. Some didn't look as if they were interested in walking anywhere at all. They just sat in the shade or kicked a lorry wheel or put their arms over each other's shoulders and talked, moving cigarettes from one side of their mouths to the other as if it was an important part of the local dialect. Once or twice a man of action came up the lane tugging at a mule loaded with cane or demijohns. A blind man with a stick found his perch against the wall outside the bar on the corner and started selling lottery tickets. Women began shouting greetings at each other from the flat *azoteas* as they hung up the laundry to dry. One or two of them competed with songs about love and hope. Rose noticed a young child come out of the doorway on the opposite side of the street and sit down on the doorstep.

After an hour of staring at the Land Rover and at the English lady in it the girl went forward and put her chin on the vehicle's window, next to where Rose had begun to read one of her husband's National Geographic magazines.

Rose smiled and offered her a biscuit which the girl grabbed and ran back to the door with. Almost immediately a woman, probably the girl's mother, snatched the biscuit out of her hands, pushed the girl inside and closed the door. Rose was just getting over the incident, without time to find an explanation for the mother's reaction, when she noticed everyone except the blind lottery paper seller had abandoned the peaceful energy of the lane. They simply scattered like leaves in a sudden gust of wind.

"Buenos días," said the grave voice.

"Buenos días," replied Rose without looking up from an article about Tibetan monks.

"Are you English?" The question did make her look out and when she did so it was into the eyes of a Guardia Civil policeman with his green uniform and black *tricornio* helmet.

Without waiting for a reply the Guardia circled the Land Rover, examining its contents through every dusty window. He stopped at the rear and held his gaze upon the purple cushions and rolled-up tartan rugs. Rose could explain about the Abercrombie tartan but what could she say about the purple cushions? The feeling of guilt about whatever crime she might have committed was nearly overwhelming but she pulled herself together by the time his face peered into hers at the window again.

"Would you like an English biscuit?" she asked. Attack is always the best form of defence.

The ploy worked. He accepted. He smiled and was most gracious in his gratitude. It was part of his duty to provoke dread. But he was just a man. He probably had a sweet wife and children and was an angel out of uniform. To keep law and order in a dictatorship, however, the custom was to make oneself feared. He was quite apologetic with his next enquiry.

"I have to ask you something, *señora*. You are not selling things, are you?"

He again directed his eyes into the back of the Land Rover and at those purple cushions and tartan rugs.

"No. Of course not," replied Rose quite sweetly. She also pretended to be indignant. It was clear the Guardia suspected contraband or black market items might be hidden under the innocent Scottish rugs.

"No. I have come with my husband. He has gone with *señores* to see a water gallery. Would you like me to open the back of the vehicle for you?" Once again, attack was the best form of defence.

"Thank you, *señora*. That will not be necessary. But we are having problems with undesirable characters coming across from Tetouan selling silk and carpets and sometimes *grifa*. Just yesterday two German hippies were caught in Alcalá purchasing *grifa* from a Moroccan."

"What is grifa?" asked Rose, knowing perfectly well that it was the local word for hashish imported from the Rif Mountains of Morocco. Her Guardia friend must have thought the question too difficult to answer because he saluted and went on his way.

Almost immediately doors and shutters began to open, the street resumed its lazy activity and the staring girl was permitted to sit on the doorstep again. Even the lizards came out to sunbathe from their holes in the walls.

Rose decided she had had enough of waiting around for her husband, policemen, mothers and staring daughters and stepped down from the Land Rover. She greeted one or two passers-by and took shelter in the only shop in the street, entering through a beaded, plastic curtain.

It was a typical local shop, with a step up off the level of the cobbles and then two more down into the cement floor of what looked like the general store. Earthenware pots stood in crazy formations in corners and traditional palm leaf, cane and willow hats and baskets adorned the white walls. Bottles of CCC-Dorada beer and green ones disguising the true colour of local wine from Chio and Arafo shared shelves with tins of tuna and sardines. Sacks of corn and beans propped up a Coca Cola sign waiting to be nailed to the wall. Canvas *lona* shoes for the *finca* workers lay in a heap next to marrows and pumpkins and squadrons of flies hovered amongst tresses of garlic and onion hung from the ceiling. Various white and cream cheeses competed for space on the wooden counter with lace, buttons and other items and a set of pale green weighing scales awaited the next customer. Next to it a cat had made itself comfortable, curled up on a box of salt fish.

A woman in strict mourning black came through a door and disappeared behind another. She was talking to herself most enthusiastically. She looks remarkably like one of Encarna's witches, thought Rose before quickly scolding herself for having had such a thought.

The man behind the counter was using a

wooden grain shovel to fill a customer's white, cloth bag with *gofio*, the local cereal mix.

"*Buenos días, señor,*" began Rose once the customer paid and departed with a polite bow. She would buy some bread and cheese and one of the earthenware pots which had caught her eye. She thought it would look pretty with some dried flowers on the verandah.

"Good morning. I'll be with you in just a minute!" The man replied in almost perfect English before his eyes met her inquisitive expression.

"Goodness. Where did you learn your English?" The last thing she had expected to find in a small lane in Granadilla was such fluent and well-pronounced English. The man looked very nice but, after all, in his dress and appearance he looked very *Canario*.

"All over the world."

"How interesting. Have you travelled a great deal?"

"Yes, I suppose so," he said, putting the shovel into a box under the counter. "Brazil, Venezuela, Bahamas, Africa, Ireland, Liverpool, London. Lots of countries. For many years I worked on an Englishman's yacht and when not I have worked in many places."

"How fascinating!" Rose was most

impressed and knew at once that she could spend the rest of the day in the shop, listening to stories and adventures.

"I am in this shop helping my sister. She became a widow last year and is suffering mental problems." That must have been the woman in black Rose had noticed.

"As soon as it is possible I shall go to London. What can I serve you, *señora?*"

"Um, some of this cheese please, and two loaves of bread. Are you going to London on business?"

"Goat's cheese? This one is from Guimar. It is smoked. This one here is fresh. We make it ourselves. Yes, in a way. I suppose I shall do business in London. I am going to claim an inheritance."

"Oh?" Rose suddenly felt a tingling sensation at the back of her neck. Her mouth tried to utter another question. It didn't come to begin with because her throat was suddenly very dry. She also implored herself not to dig deeper into the man's affairs, just in case. So she stared blankly until the man looked up and said the fatal words.

"I have a fortune waiting for me in a Bank in London!"

It was the same old story! Rose should have

just paid for some of the Guimar cheese and left the premises immediately, but she was a woman.

"Um, I don't suppose you have inherited money from Father Placido, have you?"

The man's eyebrows practically flew off his forehead and his eyes widened with evident excitement.

"Why, yes! This is amazing, *señora*. How do you know? Do you know of him?"

"No. I've just heard that he left money in a Bank in England."

"Who told you? Would you come to England with me? I will let you have half of the money."

Once again Rose tried to be prudent but her inquisitive nature and too much hanging around whilst her husband enjoyed adventures with the water men got the better of her.

"Two ladies from Santa Ursula. They told me the same as you."

"*Bah! Malditas brujas!*" The nice *Canario* with the perfect English suddenly burst forth with a series of Spanish expletives. They came spitting out of his mouth with frightening venom. The cat, which had been curled up blissfully on the box of salt fish, leapt to the floor and skidded into the darkness at the rear of the shop.

Rose followed more or less the same procedure, albeit more gracefully. She paid for the cheese and bread, thanked the man and tiptoed into the shelter of the street. The man stepped from behind the counter, following her as she fled with as much dignity as she could over the cobbles towards the Land Rover. The street was quite terrifying suddenly and Rose half expected stones to be flying over her head. Instead the man with the fortune shouted out an explanation up the street which nobody except Rose understood.

"They are my other sisters. They are mad. They are filthy witches!"

THE YOYO AND THE BUDDHA

Sadly, the beautiful old building is not there anymore. It was sold to hungry developers. They demolished it and turned it into a block of apartments using the latest in cheap, cement technology. Too late, the new apartment block is now considered an ugly and damp eyesore.

It was the end of the 1960s, when package tourism had filtered in new wealth. Cement and breeze blocks were all the rage in housing. Traditional Canary Island architecture, and mansions with high, beamed ceilings, thick, stone walls and marvellous pinewood floors were a thing of the past. My mother always said all that tearing down of beautiful old buildings reminded her of the actions of modern revolutionaries.

She was referring to the trend in certain parts of the world for statues and street names of past heroes to be brought down by regimes and emerging political groups who bitterly condemn previous forms of government. But my mother *could* be a bit outspoken at times.

Casa Reid was indeed a splendid house. It was in the very heart of Puerto de la Cruz and home to one of the longest established British firms in Tenerife. It had a lovely, cool Spanish courtyard in the middle, with ferns and a soothing fountain. A wide, polished-wood staircase invited one up to the first floor gallery. There, great double-doors, always wide open, led into large, roomy offices. Each had their own balconies with ornate, wrought-iron railings. They looked over the street and little plaza in front of the old Saint Augustine priests' school.

The company was founded in 1862 by Peter Reid, my grandfather incidentally. He had been sent to Puerto de la Cruz to establish a subsidiary for his senior cousins, the Millers of Las Palmas on the island of Grand Canary. Quite soon however, Peter decided to end the relationship and became one of the principal traders in Tenerife.

Casa Reid, as it was known locally, was also where three generations of Honorary British Vice-Consuls kept a discreet eye on their countrymen's affairs. It was indeed a splendid house and the aroma of wood varnish and Three Nuns pipe tobacco gave it a colonial air.

The ground floor was turned into one of the busiest stores in town. When they weren't engaged in other duties, faithful employees like Pepe, Antonio, Carmencita and a magnificent fellow called Baroncio would man the long, wooden counter selling anything from imported English tea and jams to sacks of fresh, local corn or potatoes and onions from the local farmers.

The whole building was always so full of vitality, good humour and old fashioned ways. One morning, however, a few years before the Labour Government introduced cuts and closed down the Vice-Consulate in Puerto de la Cruz, something rather pitiful occurred.

Noel Reid, my father, strode across the street after leaving me with Ito, the barber whose shop was across the street from his office. I was having a haircut before being packed off to prep school in England for the spring term. I heard my father greet another British resident and good friend, Ray Baillon, before disappearing into the old house. He was going up to his desk to see what letters he needed to answer. It was 1967 and Noel Reid had taken over duties from his sick brother as the last of the Honorary British Vice-Consuls in Puerto de la Cruz.

He went over to the balcony to light his pipe before sitting down at the old walnut desk. It had belonged to his grandfather a hundred years earlier and was well worn. According to my father, he was about to open the drawer where he kept his best fountain pen when he sensed there was someone else in the room.

He did not look up immediately because he was used to one of the staff entering and waiting for him to speak first.

"Do you speak English?" asked a quiet little voice.

Startled, my father spun around as if he were manning a machine-gun post. Instead of the enemy he was surprised to find a small, slightly hunched man standing against the wall under the picture of Queen Elizabeth II.

"Good morning to you!" Although he had been caught unawares my father was always polite and jovial and stood up immediately to welcome the stranger.

The hunched man didn't reply. In fact what he did quite disturbed my father. The little man put his head in his hands and began to cry.

My father was not used to seeing a man weeping. But he invited the stranger to sit down and immediately bellowed through the door for someone to bring a glass of water. After a while the man seemed to recover and, although he appeared to have some difficulty in getting his words out, my father understood that he was a retired war veteran and was looking for a friend. The man had recently arrived from Majorca and had run out of money.

This was a common plight amongst travellers, but not usually cause for a man to weep. He was not the first to ask for financial help at the Vice-Consulate and there would be no hesitation in helping the poor man out. He would be issued a small loan to keep him going for a few days or to fly him back to wherever it was he wanted to go. Meanwhile, the next step would be for the stranger to arrange to have some money sent out.

The little man introduced himself as Gerry Grimes. He claimed to have some money in the Banco Popular in Majorca. In those days there was no branch of that name in Puerto but one had recently opened in Santa Cruz. My father would not consider telling the poor man to find his own way to the capital so he told Mr Grimes he would drive him over the next morning and invited him home for lunch. Time and a little kindness offered were not scarce in those days. They were also a part of unwritten, long forgotten, British consular duties.

Inviting a total stranger to lunch was not uncommon either. Nor was it something to warn a wife about one or two years ago, especially in a Latin country. So Annette, my mother, didn't blink an eyelid when her husband arrived for lunch at *El Santísimo* with the poor little man.

Such kindness, of course, often has an effect on people. Indeed when Gerry Grimes encountered even more sympathy and warmth from the Vice-Consul's wife, his tears again poured down, this time like the Victoria Falls.

It became quite evident that the man was a psychological wreck.

After a good lunch and a nap on a rug under an avocado tree in the garden it was felt safe enough to return Mr Grimes to the house in Puerto where he had taken a room. It belonged to a middle-aged Spanish lady who made an extra *peseta* or two renting rooms out to the new breed of foreign visitor who came to stay for longer periods, especially during the winter months. Her name was Obdulia and it had been she in fact, who had sent the little man to Casa Reid.

Like most Canary Islanders, she was kind and friendly. Understandably, however, Obdulia wanted some sort of payment for the use of her room.

"*Bueno, Mister* Gerry has not paid me for two weeks and I still give him *desayuno*." She explained. She was tolerant. But enough was enough.

"*Ya está bien, hombre!*" she insisted.

My mother, Annette was well known for taking pity on strangers. I remember becoming infuriated as a teenager and unfairly accused her of paying more attention to others than she did to us. Later I realised that she was just an angel and therefore God must have given her an irresistible urge to help others.

But on this occasion she thought it wise not to interfere. Not enough time had passed since my father last blew his top. He also felt a duty to help others but he never suffered fools gladly, especially meddling women. He had been more than tolerant during the summer when my mother took in an eccentric American artist. My mother knew the intruder had rattled him to the bone when he took a camp bed to sleep in the Vice-Consulate. Well, only for three nights.

My mother had to beg the bohemian American to be on her way. Aided by help from the Luz family, owners of a vast estate known as La Quinta, just below the town of Santa Ursula, the artist was persuaded to move in to an airy little cottage above the cliffs. It worked out well, actually.

A passing bird, many years later, informed me that my mother had taken a second camp bed, cucumber sandwiches and a bottle of *cava* to the Vice-Consulate. My father and mother spent his third night in exile together. I imagine it must have been romantic and extremely funny. Those camp beds rolled over very easily.

My mother paid Obdulia what was owed out of her pocket and Mr Grimes promised to pay the rest in advance once he had received money through the bank.

The strange Englishman soon became a part of the scenery in Puerto de la Cruz. But, like anyone in his condition, he clung on like a limpet on a rock to anyone or anything offering support or kindness. Consequently he frequently returned for more.

Indeed Gerry Grimes walked up to the El Santísimo almost every day, whether there was anyone at home or not. He normally didn't accept lunch but would simply sit in the garden with a glass of water, flavoured with a slice of lemon. The servants became quite accustomed to finding him snoozing on the lawn but never got used to him picking up lizards and talking to them as if they were best friends. The odd thing is that I used to do the same when I was a little boy.

The maids also noticed that at times he seemed totally unable to speak and would just weep quietly in a corner of the drive before suddenly walking off down to Puerto again. Gerry Grimes seemed to do a lot of walking to and fro, and up and down from Puerto to Las Arenas or even further. The Englishman sometimes ended his outings abruptly before hurriedly retracing his steps. There were days when he did exactly the same walk twice or even three times. He became just another of the town's well known passers-by. Before long these up and down walks earned him a nickname. Local folk began to refer to him as *el yoyo*.

"Here comes the yoyo again," they would joke.

Then, one evening, the yoyo stopped going up and down the road. He also failed to return to Obdulia's for his evening meal.

She telephoned the Vice Consul's home. It was after ten o'clock which was a rather late hour in those days when most people still didn't have television.

"*El señor* Gerry is always here before eight. I am very worried!" she said. Obdulia genuinely *was* worried. Funnily enough she had become quite fond of her little *inglés*.

He was eventually traced to the little nun's hospital in the centre of Puerto de la Cruz. My mother, who went to see the nuns, was told that the little man with the slight hunch just turned up the previous afternoon and sat down on a bench in the courtyard. He hadn't uttered a word but began to sob. They couldn't very well turn him out so the nuns decided to bath him and put him into a bed until something could be done.

When my mother, the Vice-Consul's wife, was shown to his room Gerry Grimes was still crying his eyes out. He had also been put on a drip.

"I just asked someone to tell me the time but nobody understood so they took my clothes off and put me into this bed!" he complained.

It was decided to take the Mr Grimes to the new public hospital which was just outside the capital, Santa Cruz. My father had no alternative but to take full responsibility for the man and asked his friend, Doctor Celestino Gonzalez, to see to it that the little man was given a general check-up. They did, of course, without charge. The gesture, so often encountered in the Canary Islands, also tugged at the man's fragile emotions and he wept and wept.

What had begun with the pitiful sight of a man sobbing in my father's office had become a bit of a joke, with *el yoyo* bobbing up and down the roads. Now it turned into something quite sad.

"I'm afraid Gerry is very ill," my father said while he sat having tea with my mother under the avocado tree in the garden a day or two later.

"Oh dear. I knew there must be something behind all this. I'm going to miss him, you know," said my mother with emotion. "The lizards certainly will."

Grimes was eventually diagnosed with cancer. It was decided, on account of his fragile state of mind, that it was kindest not to inform the poor man. Nevertheless something had to be done and contact was made with his next of kin. It was his brother, Leslie Grimes in Mallorca.

Gerry's other disturbing condition was not caused by his life-ending illness. The breakdowns, the crying problem, the sudden inability to talk and the long, drifting walks, the yoyo's brother explained, were symptoms of a posttraumatic stress disorder, often referred to as shell shock suffered during the war.

It was arranged, therefore, to persuade Mr Grimes to return to England to a war veteran's hospice. His brother made the arrangements. It was all very quick.

Gerry Grimes promised to come back because he had grown fond of the kindness received by the islanders. He never did, of course. But he did leave my parents some documents and a large oil painting of a sitting Buddha for safekeeping.

Before he died the little Englishman wrote a brief letter to my mother. The writing wasn't very good but it was quite clear that he understood why he would not be talking to his lizards in her garden again. The last sentence opened my mother's own floodgates and her own tears left inky smudges over the airmail paper.

"Dear Annette. You have been my angel. You are a treasure of faith and fortitude. I want you to keep my Buddha. I know he will find peace with you."

The painting of the sitting Buddha was signed simply GRIMES. We always assumed

the strange little Englishman with the scars of
war inside his head had been the artist. Until
one day in 1978. A package arrived for my
father. It contained an exact replica of the
sitting Buddha and it had been painted by
Gerry's brother, Leslie Grimes. My parents
discovered that he had been a well-known
wartime cartoonist and he had made his home
on the Mediterranean island of Mallorca in
1952. He painted many local scenes and sold
well at local galleries. I understand he painted a
number of identical sitting Buddha, but that
doesn't matter. What is important to me is that
he wanted my father to have a copy as a token
of gratitude for taking pity on his brother.

This time it was my father who was seen to
shed a tear. Both my parents now had their
own sitting Buddha.

A few years later a new parson was required
for All Saints Church in Puerto de la Cruz. A
very thoughtful and jolly reverend soon came
to Tenerife for an interview and to see whether
the position suited him. Towards the end of
his visit he was invited to lunch at El
Santísimo. It was a rainy, late October day.

After lunch they took coffee in the study. Over the fire place hung one of the paintings of the sitting Buddha. It is still there.

"I've got the original of that painting" insisted the Reverend, clearly taken aback by the familiar, peaceful image in front of him.

"Do you know?" he remarked to his wife, "I think we are going be very happy on this island."

ILLEGAL IMMIGRANT

There is a statue, just past the old fishing mole in the town of Garachico on the Canary Island of Tenerife. It catches the eye as one drives out of the port towards the western towns of Los Silos and Buenavista in what is known as the low island.

The statue stands on what they call the broken rock. It is a good place from where to gaze back over the rooftops of the town or out to the swelling Atlantic. The statue is of a man, determined and anxious. He carries pieces of luggage and is about to leave the island of Tenerife for the promised continent of South America. The sculptor has left a gaping hole where the man's heart should be. He leaves it behind in his beloved Garachico where there is also a young girl with a broken heart.

The statue was erected in 1990 and is a monument to the island's emigrants. They left in their thousands, first in the 19th century and then especially in the early part of the 20th century, to escape poverty, starvation and political persecution.

The statue could well be the image of Domingo. He was twenty three when the need to find a better life and to help his impoverished family willed him to listen to a man called Ortega. He could find Domingo a way across the Atlantic to Cuba or Venezuela, like so many other islanders before him.

The Canary Islanders had suffered the consequences of the Great War. Then, just as exports and trade began to bring fresh hope, at least to the wealthy classes, the Spanish Civil War brought savagery and bitterness. When the Second World War erupted, all hope for trade with Europe was lost. German U-Boats mercilessly hunted down merchant ships passing by the strategically-placed Canary Islands and they became almost completely cut off from the rest of the world.

It took Domingo nearly two years to raise the 4,500 pesetas demanded for arranging his passage. It was a small fortune in 1947 and emigration was still considered illegal. Ortega and one or two other silent operators had discovered there was a profit to be made from the needs of others to escape poverty or political repression in the early days of the Franco dictatorship.

Domingo was told to go to a house in an alley called Venus which led from the church of Santa Ana down to the small fortress of San Miguel, above the volcanic rock pools. The address had once been adorned with the frills of wealth but even here there were signs that the years had been cruel. There was money, of course, but it was earned from the illegal business of contraband and exporting human beings. Therefore wealth was not flaunted for fear of being found out.

There was a metal sign above the door of the house in the alley with the words and numbers *London Assurance 1720*. Wealth and insurance had once come from years of trade and business with Great Britain.

Domingo lifted the iron door knocker and knocked twice. He had been told to act naturally if questioned by a patrolling member of the law. He was simply there to do business.

But the sound of the knocker echoed down the lane and Domingo found it almost impossible to act as if nothing strange was going on and he glanced nervously up and down the cobbles while his hands fiddled incessantly inside empty jacket pockets. He knocked for a second time, this time more timidly. He was about to leave, almost with relief, when he heard a voice.

"*Momento. Ya va,*" it said, acknowledging his presence and informing him that someone was on their way.

After another, uncomfortable wait a small postigo opened in the wooden shutter above him. An old woman's face peered down into the alley and then immediately closed the wooden flap again without saying a word.

After a further delay the big front door opened and Ortega led Domingo into a stone courtyard and up a wide pinewood staircase to the gallery above. Domingo noticed the old woman who had peeped down at him disappear with a candle behind a door at the end of the corridor. Another doorway led into Ortega's *despacho*, a high ceilinged room with a round table in the middle. It was covered untidily with ledgers and papers and a couple of silver candlesticks were being used as paperweights. Domingo thought the smell of damp and dust was almost as unpleasant as Ortega himself and he very nearly didn't hand over the small, cloth parcel containing the money.

But he did and, just after mass on the following Sunday evening, Domingo began to break Marta's heart. It would not take long, he said. He swore to return a rich man. They would marry. She promised to wait for him.

Marta's heart finally broke five weeks later when Domingo departed. First he grabbed a lift into the port of Santa Cruz and thence took a small freighter carrying fruit to the port of La Luz in Las Palmas, the capital of the island of Grand Canary. There he was to go to another backstreet address where he would wait, together with others, for two fishing sloops. These would set sail, as if on any other fishing trip, towards the African coast. On the outward journey the sloops would be weighed down with their human cargo. On their return they would bring back tuna and other fish, cut open and salted for preservation, for the fish stalls in Las Palmas.

It was off the Jandía Peninsula, to the south of Fuerteventura, the closest island to Africa, where the rendezvous had been arranged with the other vessel contracted to sail them to the Americas.

Fuerteventura was one of the least populated of the Canary Islands and only a handful of people lived anywhere near Jandía, that desolate, windswept stretch of land to the south. It was far enough away from patrols to make it safe.

There have been a thousand stories told about Jandía. The possibility of a secret German base during WW2 still wraps a mysterious veil around the peninsula. Today it has become a haven for tourists, with its never-ending white sand beaches and wind for modern windsurfers. In 1947 it was still remote enough for the clandestine activity organised by Ortega in Garachico. The Jandía Peninsula is on the remains of an ancient volcanic caldera whose other half is under the sea. A million years ago there was probably a separate island. Now it is joined to the rest of the elongated island by a sandy isthmus known as The Wall.

As Domingo discovered over the next weeks, he would encounter many a wall during his quest for a better life away from the island of Tenerife.

□□□□□□□□□

In September, 1938, when the Spanish civil war appeared to be coming to a slow and tortuous end, the international brigades which had fought alongside the Spanish Republicans were disbanded. This included the British Battalion into which brave, idealistic and possibly innocent volunteers had been seduced by the call of communism, anti-fascism and glory. Now, with many comrades buried deep in Spanish soil, the dream was over and 305 survivors returned to London's Victoria Station on 7th December. They were given a hero's welcome and met by Clement Attlee and Stafford Cripps, senior Labour Party politicians, among others.

But not all British volunteers returned. A handful decided to risk not being captured by Franco's victors and certain death against a wall by firing squad. One or two remained because they had fallen for a lovely Spanish *señorita*. Others because they just didn't want to face consequences back home.

One of these was Percy Colvert. He came from a wealthy, very Conservative family in Hampshire and was educated at Harrow. But he turned red, as so many young did, after dropping out from university. He was not a good student, ridiculed tradition and gave his family hell. Friends said he was never a part of the crowd.

But he began to make enough of that capitalist money he so despised by wheeling and dealing in boats and marine spares along the south coast of England. Percy Colvert had been doing quite well for himself when he was enticed by the quixotic call of duty in Spain.

Having slipped through the Nationalist net after the Battle of Jarama he made his way to Barcelona before heading southwest. Dodging all obstacles he made a living doing all sorts of odd jobs. He found himself doing much the same as he did in England on the Spanish Mediterranean coast and opened a marine store. Quite soon Percy purchased a small vessel with which he made a fortune ferrying contraband and people between the Spanish North African colonies, Morocco, Gibraltar and the Peninsula.

The bitter Civil War was at an end but the Second World War was just beginning. Both Spain and French-controlled Morocco remained neutral states and there was a fortune to be made by any experienced wheeler-dealer like Percy Colvert. He also found a lucrative business ferrying political refugees escaping persecution from the Nationalists in Spain out of the country after the Civil War. In 1943 he purchased an absolute beauty of a ship for a song.

The vessel, a two-masted yacht, had been left behind by a foreign millionaire in the early 1930s. She was 123ft long with a beam of 24.5ft and had begun life as a fishing schooner off Iceland so she was a sturdy seagoing vessel. The name on the rounded stern was Capriccio and her bow was adorned by a sculpted figurehead of a woman in seductive pose. Colvert rather liked that.

In 1947 Percy was approached by a gentleman in Barcelona. Could he sail sixty five refugees across the Atlantic? That was over double the number of passengers he normally ferried clandestinely in the Mediterranean but he could not refuse. His cut was 2,500 pesetas a head. The money was just too good in those difficult, uncertain days.

It was a risk worth taking. Yes, he could do it. The passengers would not have a comfortable ride and he would need to undertake certain modifications below deck to make room on the Capriccio. But who cared. It was business. Besides, he was acting against the fascist dictatorship in Spain.

Towards the end of July and in spite of the strong, predominant north easterly trade wind, Colvert eased the Capriccio, with the help of her twin Perkins engines turning over gently, towards the coast of Fuerteventura. He crept as close as he dared into the calmer waters of a small bay three miles east of Jandía Point. There was no moon and the night was pitch-black but he could clearly make out the surf on a white beach and the darker shapes in the mountains above.

As he had stipulated, one beam of light, sustained for five seconds, was the signal that the two fishing sloops from Las Palmas were approaching his position. He replied with three rapid flashes. He was ready to take on the remaining twenty eight passengers from the Canary Islands. Aboard already, and having embarked at Algeciras, were his four crew members and thirty six Spanish émigrés from varying backgrounds, men and women. Only two actually revealed themselves as political refugees. Most, like Domingo from Garachico, just sought to make a living, to escape economic misery in Spain.

The sloops took turns to nudge alongside Capriccio's port side. Nobody made a sound as they were helped aboard. Their faces betrayed exhaustion from the past few days in hiding and fear. The tension in the air was unbearable. They all knew the consequences of being caught. What they were doing was forbidden and punishable under the strict controls typical of dictatorships with prison or, in some cases, execution.

Colvert breathed deep as he turned Capriccio about and pushed the throttles forwards. He glanced over his shoulder and watched the fishing boats head south east towards African waters.

Shortly afterwards, clear of the sand dunes and the rocks to the west, Colvert told his crew to unfurl the sails while his passengers found what little room they could. Most went below decks to escape the cold and spray, squeezing in with those who had boarded Capriccio in the Spanish peninsula. Some found shelter on deck as best they could.

Colvert closed down the engines when the sails began to catch the first hint of the Elysian trade winds a mile to the south of the rendezvous position. But suddenly, as he turned the wheel to point Capriccio in a south westerly direction to clear Jandía Point they heard a muffled thud. They saw the lights of a vessel approaching from around the point. It was a Spanish patrol boat. It had fired a warning shot and was approaching fast.

"Halt in the name of Spain!" a loud hailer threatened.

"Identify yourself!"

The boat was going to cut them off. They had been found out. Colvert swore and prayed under the same breath. He recognised fear in the faces around him. He felt death as he hadn't since the Battle of Jarama.

"Surrender at once!" ordered the rough voice in the loudspeaker.

"Surrender? *La puta de tu madre!*" replied a member of the crew defiantly from the darkness on Capriccio just as the full force of the north easterly filled the sails and the schooner suddenly surged ahead. More thudding shots were heard and another shout through the loud hailer threatened again. But the lights of the patrol boat began to fade and it lost interest as Colvert steered south into bigger seas.

Domingo was one of the passengers who decided to find shelter on deck, wrapping himself under canvas. He knew they were safe, out of range and on their way. He closed his eyes. But it became hard, very hard.

□□□□□□□□□

Capriccio was just one of many vessels which became known in the Canary Islands as the phantom boats. Some departed under the cover of darkness and were never seen or heard of again. There is a disturbing similarity with those who risk all in the Mediterranean, escaping from Africa or the Middle East in the early 21st century.

Thousands were tempted to pay a small fortune for a passage on those phantom boats. Most were old fishing craft based in the Canary Islands with specially adapted rigging. On a vessel with room for fifty passengers space would be found for as many as two hundred and eighty. They would be packed in the hold, lying down and squeezed together like tinned sardines. The voyage, pushed by the trade winds and currents, could take as much as forty days. Conditions were inhuman. Many passengers, if they were lucky enough to reach American shores alive, arrived without documents or money. Most were detained and held in immigration centres until some wealthy landowner came by to choose his cheap and obedient labour force. In many ways it resembled the African slave trade.

Those on Capriccio could consider themselves lucky. There were only sixty five passengers and they were not arrested on arrival in Venezuela. But the journey had been equally squalid and dangerous.

One of the crew Percy Colvert had specially chosen for helping them make the transatlantic voyage was Ander Undurraga, a tough looking man from the Basque region of Spain. He claimed to have owned his own trawler before the Civil War and that he had sailed well into the north Atlantic. Colvert took him on as a navigator and first mate and handed over Capriccio to him in the early hours of that first night out from Fuerteventura.

The problem with Undurraga began early the next morning. *El Felino*, a man in his forties who had been with Colvert since his first contraband boat in the Mediterranean, woke up the English captain.

"We're not going well *Señor Perce*," he said.
"*Que pasa* Juan?"

Colvert stirred quickly. Juan, the one they called *the feline* on account of his skinny complexion and trapeze-artist ability to climb and jump every inch of the boat, sounded breathless.

"It is morning. We have sun portside. We go south, not west!"

He was right and some of the passengers on the deck had begun to murmur. Domingo was one of them. They were indeed sailing south, if not south east. The sun was definitely rising on the port side when it should have been directly behind Capriccio if she was heading west.

Undurraga had lied. One thing was simple coastal navigation, following the coast of Africa, past the island of Lanzarote and then on south along the length of Fuerteventura. But he hadn't a clue about open-sea celestial navigation. The Basque, who also appeared to have been drinking during his watch, broke down. He said he was a political refugee and desperate to avoid capture.

Percy Colvert felt no sympathy. He did not want the man aboard his ship. He was furious with himself for letting the Basque cheat him about his navigation skills. But drinking while on watch was unforgiveable. He would have to dump the man.

They would turn about and sail north, even towards Las Palmas if necessary and risk capture, in order to drop the Basque in a remote bay somewhere. It was not going to be easy explaining to the passengers or to the rest of the crew why he had taken the decision to turn back. An alternative would be to sail towards the African coast and leave Undarraga to an even more uncertain fate. But how could he justify that without telling everyone about the Basque?

Colvert took Ander Undurraga aside and informed him that he would be put ashore. The man's response was a murderous glare. Colvert had witnessed a similar look of insanity, fear and hatred in the Civil War when Spaniard killed fellow Spaniard and he too felt fear as the Basque turned angrily past the wheel and stepped down below deck.

Colvert did not want to alarm the passengers further. If they knew the truth they would surely lynch the northerner. He took *el felino* aside and told him to inform everyone that they had a minor problem and would need to carry out repairs on Grand Canary before continuing.

Juan was just about to inform passengers and crew of his decision when Undurraga appeared on deck again. This time he held a standard Astra 400 pistol and pointed the weapon at the nearest passenger.

"If we go back to Las Palmas I will kill everyone, one by one!" he threatened.

There was no option and Colvert knew it. So the English captain and owner of Capriccio agreed with Undurraga that he would not return to Las Palmas but told him that he must remain on deck, and at all times at the bow of the schooner. With no more ado Colvert pointed Capriccio's bow west and kept the morning sun astern. The Basque would calm down once the drink wore off. He could be dealt with later, quietly and another way.

It turned out that Ander Undurraga was more than just a political refugee. He was wanted for various murders in Navarra and would undoubtedly face the death penalty if the Spanish authorities got hold of him.

Over the next two days Percy Colvert grasped enough navigational skills to feel confident enough. He used Capriccio's chronometer and the sun at dawn and at dusk to calculate his position. He told *el felino* to keep the morning sun behind them at all times. Logic told him that they would meet the Americas somewhere. It was instinctive navigation. But the sculpted figurehead of Capriccio must have seduced the gods because the first shores they sighted were of their promised land.

Despite having been nearly wrecked by a tropical storm between Trinidad and Tobago the schooner, which lost the top of her foremast, was spotted twenty six days after leaving Jandía. Colvert had been hugging the north coast of Venezuela. She was escorted in to the port of La Guaira by a National Guard vessel which looked as if it might once have been a British torpedo boat.

The officer who came aboard to pilot the phantom boat into port nearly puked when he inspected below deck. In a report later that day he wrote, "*the conditions aboard were lamentable. These illegal immigrants, including six women and two children, were famished and dirty and their clothes were in shreds. The hold was like a pool of vomit and the smell was unbearable.*"

It was just as Domingo from Garachico would always describe the voyage. Many passengers suffered severe sea sickness. Those in the hold below decks relieved themselves behind a wooden partition and when they couldn't get there in time, clambered over other passengers and vomited over each other. They soon all had lice. The acid from the vomit and seawater stung and burnt them and the women used filthy rags or bits of clothes torn off with which to clean themselves. In a matter of days Capriccio stunk like a sewer.

Seven passengers didn't make it. They were either lost overboard or died sick and were buried at sea. Ander, the Basque, disappeared on the third night into the Atlantic. Nobody asked any questions.

Domingo found work on a sugar cane plantation in Yaracuy State. But Venezuela was an emerging gold mine and he had not left his sweetheart to work as a slave. So, after receiving his first wage he took a bus to Caracas, the booming capital. He worked in a bar and made extra money at night washing big, imported American Cadillacs and Pontiacs. Domingo soon realised that in a growing economy there was money to be made in transport. It didn't take him long to save enough *bolívares* to buy himself a second hand Chevrolet truck. Unlike Percy Colvert, Domingo transported anything except humans. Within five years he owned a fleet of twenty lorries and employed fellow immigrants from the Canary Islands to transport goods throughout the country.

Nobody knows what became of the English Captain, incidentally. Perhaps he replaced the mast on Capriccio and offered his services throughout the Caribbean islands. Maybe he drank *mojitos* with fellow Republican, Ernest Hemmingway at the *Bodeguita del Medio* in Havana. Who knows?

Domingo made more than a fortune. But he never kept his promise to Marta. Instead he married a girl whose family had gone to

Venezuela from the Canary island of La Palma in 1917. Sadly she took her own life when she was 52. Viperous tongues spoke of Domingo's infidelities being the cause of growing bouts of depression. They had no children.

In 1996 Domingo, the illegal immigrant, decided to become an émigré again, back to the island of Tenerife. He had grown tired of corrupt politicians and attempted coups. He also feared Venezuela, his land of opportunity, would disintegrate into an impoverished chaos controlled by megalomaniacs. He was right.

Over the years he had slipped considerable sums out of the country. It seemed to be what everyone did. He invested in companies in the USA and Europe. Hence much of his personal fortune had been slowly but surely transferred to accounts in New York and London. Domingo was a millionaire.

Before leaving Venezuela, he discreetly and generously saw to it that his companies were taken over by cooperatives of loyal employees. Although there were no members of his family left alive in the Canary Islands there was nothing for him to stay for in South America.

When Domingo returned to Garachico he found that Marta had not kept her promise to him either. She had not waited for him. He discovered that she no longer lived in the small village of San Pedro, overlooking the tiny beach and old fishing port. Further enquiries told him that she had married into a wealthy Garachico family. Her husband had died some years earlier. She had six children and a whole troop of grandchildren.

Marta had married a gentleman by the name of Pablo Ortega. Domingo could not believe it. His sweetheart had married the eldest son of that unpleasant little man, Ortega, the owner of the house with the London Assurance Company plaque above the door in Garachico, the one who had taken 4,500 pesetas off him for his passage across the Atlantic. Initially he had a feeling of betrayal, as if he had a right to Marta's life. It took Domingo one or two days to unwind and reflect on how lucky he had been and that Ortega had in fact helped him escape. Had it not been for the unpleasant little man, he would not have made a fortune in Venezuela.

It took Domingo almost two weeks more to find the courage to call on Marta. She was still alive and, like himself, in her early seventies.

He asked the young taxi driver outside the lavish Botánico Hotel in Puerto de la Cruz to take him to Garachico. It was one of those beautiful, clear September mornings. The north coast, under the cliffs, looked spectacular. The sea, beyond the bananas and the dragon trees, was like a watercolour of gentle summer waves. Families with kids would be flocking down to the beaches for the last of the long, Spanish summer holiday.

There were already children splashing about in the rock pools of Garachico when the taxi dropped Domingo off just next to the San Miguel fortress. He put on his straw hat and walked slowly across the road, thanking cars for stopping with a wave of his walking stick.

After passing a coffee shop called Le Patissier, very French for the island, he thought, Domingo turned left into the alley called *Venus*. At the top, just below the steps which led up to the church of Santa Ana and under a scarlet bougainvillea, he stopped. The house of Ortega was just as he remembered it in 1947. Perhaps it was even more run down. It still had the metal sign above the door which said London Assurance, 1720. The only difference was that the house had been given a number.

Domingo knocked on the door of N° 3.

This time he didn't have to wait long. The

postigo in the brown shutter above opened and a little girl's face shone down at him.

"*Hola!*" it said cheerfully.

"*Hola!*" he replied, lifting his hat with the stick.

Before he could introduce himself the little girl had turned her face round and shouted to someone inside.

"*Abuela*, Grandma. There's an old man at the door!" she announced before promptly disappeared, letting the flap close behind her.

This time there was a longer wait before the postigo opened again. An ageing woman looked down at Domingo. Neither he nor she uttered a word. They couldn't. The old lady was Marta, his sweetheart. The shutter closed.

A few moments later there was the sound of a bolt being moved behind the door and it opened slowly. Marta stood there, dressed all in traditional mourning black. She greeted him with old, grey eyes. But they twinkled with happiness.

"I've been expecting you for a long time!" she said before opening her arms. They both wept in each other's arms, but the love returned. It was different, but it was there.

A MISSED CALL

The sound of the generator faded at last. The lights dimmed and all was quiet except for a dog barking somewhere in the distance. It was ten o'clock and Noel Reid lay under no more than the white sheet of the hotel bed.

It was warm and sticky, almost tropical. But he felt refreshed after a late evening swim out around the anchored fishing boats and a cold trickle of water from the temperamental hotel shower. A sea breeze helped soothe the summer air and flirted with the curtain, letting the moon peep through. Before closing his eyes he whispered *I love you* to it. It was a custom he had never failed to keep and which had begun in those early love-letter days whenever he was away from his beloved wife, Annette, as if she too might be talking to him through the moon.

But it was July 1964 and at that time of the night, apart from the dog and the waves on the shore, there was almost complete silence in the fishing village of Los Cristianos.

The Hostal Reverón was the only place offering a room in the area. It was family-run and quite adequate. Electricity was produced by that diesel generator and although there was no hot water the rooms were spotless and the service amicable. It was all there was, all one expected and all one needed in those days.

Los Cristianos, with its yellow beach and little fishing port, was paradise after a day visiting the farmers in the barren and dusty south of Tenerife.

Noel Reid had returned to the family home in Puerto de la Cruz on the northern coast of the island ten years earlier. He had spent almost thirty years making a small fortune growing tea in Africa. Now, with only a small fruit farm to his name above the village of Ravelo, in the northern hills of Tenerife, he spent most of his spare time experimenting with onion seed and buying tomatoes for a Scottish fruit importer.

He enjoyed touring around the tomato plantations. He liked to make sure he got the best of the season's crop for his client. He also took great pleasure in sharing life's experiences with tomato farmers on the southern slopes of Tenerife from Arafo to Chio. They became very fond of *don Noel* and always welcomed him with their own wines and cheeses. Theirs were very civilised business meetings. Life was easy going.

Sometimes, if he was planning to spend longer in *el sur*, as the south of the island was called, his wife would accompany him. Long before the roads became more than dusty tracks a trip to the south of Tenerife was considered an adventure. Instead of spending a night or two at the Hostal Reverón they camped on a barren piece of land close to the sea, with the stars and the moon lighting up the southern mountains. Sometimes they would bed down in the back of their Land Rover and sometimes in a tent pitched close by. It was most romantic and reminded them of their younger days in Africa, under the moonlight and on the banks of a river with the Chimanimani Mountains behind them. Today that barren piece of land in Tenerife is known as Las Americas, the largest and most populated tourist resort in the Canary Islands.

Noel was too tired to do anything about the familiar sound of a mosquito homing in on his blood and just covered his head with the sheet for protection. Without the mosquito nets they had in Africa it was the next best form of defence. The waves, slapping surf on the yellow beach, soon rocked him into a deep sleep.

□□□□□□□□□

Earlier that same evening, on the other side of the island ridge, another British citizen walked briskly along the San Telmo seafront in Puerto de la Cruz. Once or twice he stopped and looked back as if he might be followed. He passed the church and the Monopol and Marquesa Hotels and continued down to *Plaza del Charco*. It was the main square in front of the fishing port and where the red *guaguas* and black taxis waited lazily for custom.

"To Caledonia, *por favor. Rápido.*"

Caledonia was the house of *don Rio*, the British Vice-Consul in Puerto de la Cruz. He also happened to be Noel Reid's younger brother.

A beautiful villa set in extensive gardens and shaded by jacaranda trees, cypresses and avocado trees, Caledonia stood on the edge of a volcanic mound next to the Grand Taoro Hotel. The drive meandered past roses and a well-maintained vegetable garden to the front door steps. It was a jewel of a property which Rio Reid and his wife Jean had built in 1936. The view over the Martiánez Bay was spectacular although, where there were once banana plantations right up to the sea, by 1964 the hotel boom was beginning to show its rectangular, flat rooftops and concrete structures. Soon after Rio Reid died in 1969 the property was bought by a Belgian for his own wife. It was no surprise when they turned the house into a charming café called *Risco*

Bello, the beautiful rock, with water gardens overlooking the town.

The scent of jasmine blossom cascaded down from the creeper over the front door where Berta, the housekeeper, beckoned the visitor into the hall. She had seen him once before at one of Caledonia's cocktail parties although he had not been invited again. He was one of the new English arrivals. His name was Shouldham and he had come to Tenerife accompanying his mother. She had bought an apartment in town. The poor man gave private maths lessons for a time in Puerto de la Cruz and was regarded a bit of an alcoholic.

He needed to speak to the Vice-Consul with a matter of urgency. The Vice Consulate offices down in Puerto were closed for the evening and that is why he had come to Mr Reid's private residence.

Berta, who had learnt to speak a reasonable amount of English, was most kind and invited the gentleman through the sitting room and out onto the verandah.

"Please wait here *señor*. I shall ask if *don Río* can attend to you. He is very *enfermo* today," she said and disappeared before the Englishman could say anything.

A maid in a grey dress and white apron

brought the English gentleman a small jug of lemonade. He did not touch it. A whisky or a gin would have been more appropriate. Nor did he sit down. Instead Mr Shouldham lit a cigarette. The view of the perfectly manicured lawn and glorious pink and white frangipanis were of no interest to him as he paced up and down the verandah taking long drags on his Rothmans. There was no time for Canary Island charm and serenity. His was a matter of urgency and he was in a right old state of nerves.

Walter Reid, known as *Rio*, apologised for taking so long and for his attire. He wore a purple and cream striped dressing gown over plain, blue pyjamas. Indeed, he did not look well and yet his small blue eyes were sharp and smiling behind gold-rimmed, half-moon spectacles.

"How can I help you, Mr Shouldham?"

"Napoleon! He's down at the lido. I'm sure it was him," proclaimed Mr Shouldham.

"Um, I do beg your pardon. What are you talking about? Who is this *Napoleon*?"

The only Napoleons the Vice-Consul had ever heard of were Bonaparte and the leader of a gang of cats who used to attack barges on the English canals in the Bill Badger stories which he used to read to his nephew.

"That's his nickname. I can't remember his real name. But I'm certain I've seen his face in the papers. If it isn't him I swear I'll go to church on Sunday."

The Vice-Consulate was well aware of Mr Shouldham's drinking problems but on this occasion he appeared to be reasonably sober. The man was just in a dreadful state of excitement. Nevertheless his story did make sense. One of Britain's most wanted criminals, a member of the Great Train Robbery gang was often referred to as *Napoleon*.

So Mr Reid listened, his calm demeanour almost fending off the informant's near hysteria.

"Thank you very much for taking the trouble, Mr Shouldham. You have done absolutely the right thing and I shall inform the local authorities immediately."

Berta brought the Vice-Consul a headed sheet of cream writing paper and a Parker fountain pen. He scribbled a few lines in Spanish. He folded the paper and placed it in an envelope, addressing it for the attention of Capitán Galvan, *Guardia Civil*. Underlined, in capital letters, he wrote *URGENTE – CONFIDENCIAL*.

"I'm asking Andrés, my chauffeur, to take you wherever you wish but I would be grateful if on the way you would drop this letter off at the Civil Guard headquarters. Thank you very much indeed for your swift, responsible and commendable actions."

As soon as Mr Shouldham departed the seventy year old Vice-Consul retired back to his bed. Soon, he thought, he was going to have to hand over the business of looking after British affairs to someone who was more active, and not as very ill as he knew he was.

But he did make one last call. An operator at the telephone exchange put him through to Captain Galvan, chief of the Civil Guard police HQ in the Orotava Valley. After brief pleasantries Mr Reid told the policeman that Shouldham was on his way and would provide more information. However, on account of his failing health Mr Reid suggested they should ask his brother Noel to represent him in making the citizen's arrest. The alternative would have been to contact his senior, Her Majesty's Consul in Santa Cruz. Unfortunately, Mr Fox was currently on a visit to Madrid.

Mr Shouldham's information was indeed a matter of importance. If true it could mean the capture of one of Britain's most wanted criminals.

What Captain Galván didn't admit to the British Vice-Consul during their brief conversation was that they had been aware that a suspected British criminal was on the island for a couple of days. In fact the suspect already had a trail on him and one of Galván's men had been observing him that very afternoon drinking with two other foreigners on the terrace at the San Telmo lido bar.

But arresting the suspect was not a piece of cake. A one hundred-year old extradition treaty did exist between Spain and Great Britain. On paper. But it was not working and when it did extradition requests were dealt with at snail pace, on both sides. The same applied to simple requests for putting handcuffs on a wanted criminal. Each country's different legal systems could not come to terms with complicated applications for action to be taken on behalf of each other's police forces. The common way around the problem, also keeping political involvement out of the legal jigsaw, was to resort to a citizen's arrest, wherever it was possible. It was much quicker and, however unorthodox, possibly more efficient and discreet.

Once the local Spanish authorities had been

informed of the presence or of the imminent arrival of the suspected English criminal Captain Galván had been ordered to keep an eye open. In fact he had taken immediate action. With a description of his target he had sent officers in plain clothes to make enquiries. One had been visiting all the hotels in Puerto. The other was to sniff around at the San Telmo lido where another anonymous informant had apparently also spotted *Napoleon*.

Galván wanted no fuss, just a quiet arrest. No need to disturb the growing population of innocent holiday-makers.

The plan was to locate the man and to then accompany Noel Reid to proceed with the detention of the English criminal. The chief was looking forward to it and he knew the Vice-Consul's brother would relish the moment.

Captain Galván picked up the telephone receiver to the right of his desk.

"*Buenas tardes, Central,*" he greeted the girl at the telephone exchange.

"*Hola mi Capitán,*" replied the operator. "How are you? How happy I am to talk to you."

"*Muy buenas,* Josefina. Look, no time for

chatter. Put me through to *Don Noel.*"

The telephone exchanges in Tenerife in the 1960s were still manually operated by telephonists. Because they had to put a call through and wait for a reply they could easily listen in on conversations. They invariably did. Consequently they knew more about what was going on than the most brilliant of private detectives. They also often knew the movements of people like Noel Reid.

"*Don Noel no está en casa,*" Nina informed the police chief.

"He isn't at home. He left early this morning."

"Is he on the island?"

"Oh yes, he is in *el sur*. At lunch time he was in Arafo. He spoke to his wife from the telephone exchange there," she added. Josefina had herself connected Noel Reid with his wife that very mid-day.

"Well, put me through to *Doña Anita.*"

"*Momentito* Capitán."

Josefina plugged the Civil Guard telephone into the appropriate jack for the other Reid house. A moment or two later the black, 1950s design French telephone began to ring in the hall at *El Santisimo*.

"Um, hello?" answered Annette Reid in her

familiar manner and then froze when the Captain introduced himself.

"No. There's nothing to be concerned about, Doña Anita. I am sorry to disturb you. But we require your husband's assistance on a very important matter. We understand that he is in the south. Do you know when he will return or where we can find him?"

"I see. Well, my husband told me he would be coming back to the north tomorrow evening via Chio. He was in Arafo for lunch today and then I think he said he was going to Granadilla."

"Do you know who he was going to see in Granadilla? Galván insisted.

"I'm sorry. No, I don't. But he was going to have lunch with Don Eduardo Curbelo in Arafo. He might know."

"And tonight? Will don Noel be sleeping in the Land Rover or at Los Cristianos?"

Annette Reid was taken aback at how much the police chief knew about her husband's habits and told Galván rather stiffly that she didn't know. She was always willing to help the Civil Guard but enough was enough.

"I am so sorry Capitán Galván. I'm sure you know that wives, especially in Spain, don't know absolutely everything that their husbands get up to." She kicked herself for losing her cool and tried to make amends.

"He very much likes the Hostal Reverón in Los Cristianos."

"*Muchas gracias, señora*," the policeman replied, knowing very well that Noel Reid was a frequent guest there.

"Thank you very much. I am grateful to you. Please accept my apologies for disturbing you." Galván was exquisite in his manner.

A primitive, manual telephone exchange system in Tenerife was installed towards the end of the 19th century. By the 1930s there was a complex but efficient system of wooden telegraph poles and communication wires stretching all around the island. They communicated district telephone exchanges operated mainly by bright young ladies. They had all been required to pass rigorous tests to qualify as a telephonist. It was a sought after occupation in a world where few women worked for a living. If they did it was either the telephone exchange, on the terraces picking tomatoes, digging up home-grown potatoes and onions or sitting at home waiting to become a wife.

"*Entonces qué?* Do you want me to find don Noel or not?" asked Josefina mischievously after Annette Reid hung up the telephone. She had listened in on every word.

"Yes. Arafo. Immediately. With Don Eduardo Curbelo. If he isn't there then put me through to the Guardia Civil in Granadilla."

The chase was on but it was slow business. Getting a line was not always immediate and Josefina's wire route to track down Don Noel meant being passed from one district telephone exchange to another where her colleagues would then plug in the line to the next appropriate jack on the wooden boxes in front of them.

There were other complications. The telephonists were loyal servants and professional. But they were also human, women and Spanish. Therefore an opportunity to chat and compare gossip was never frowned upon, especially when there was no supervisor. They could also be distracted and therefore absent without leave from the vital communications apparatus.

As it happened there was only one girl at the Arafo exchange that evening. Her name was *Cande* and she was twenty two. She had blossomed into a very attractive young lady and she knew it. Consequently she never missed an opportunity to flirt with boys prowling Santi's Bar on the other side of the sloping street.

When Josefina plugged in, hoping to have a quick natter with Cande before being put through to Don Eduardo, the Arafo telephonist was being distracted by a tall, handsome lad oozing charm from outside the bar.

Josefina tried once more before reporting to Captain Galván that there was a problem with Arafo. It had been a missed call.

The next connection was Granadilla. The words *immediate* or *urgent* had little effect on a sleepy Atlantic island in the 1960s and the hours passed. By the time Don Noel was tracked down to Los Cristianos it was midnight and no time to disturb anyone.

□□□□□□□□□

The first put-put of a fishing boat leaving its moorings in Los Cristianos Bay awakened Noel Reid. It was six o'clock and he took a cold shower. He looked forward to breakfast. The Hostal Reverón always provided a huge bowl of coffee and milk and plenty of bread, jams and cheeses. He was just packing his overnight bag before going down to the dining room when there was a timid knock on the hotel room door.

"Don Noel, *soy* Eugenio," said the voice behind the door. "They want to talk to you!"

With just the white hotel towel around his waist he opened the door to find Eugenio, the porter. Behind him in the narrow passage were two Guardia Civil policemen. It was

Lieutenant Herrero and Sergeant Peréstolo from Granadilla, the police HQ in the south of the island. He knew their faces well as they had often met during their patrols on the dusty southern roads.

"Forgive our disturbing you Don Noel but there is a matter of great urgency," whispered the senior but younger and less experienced of the two of the two policemen. Before Noel Reid had time to imagine that something dreadful had happened at home Sergeant Peréstolo intervened in his rougher, more provincial manner.

"We've got a *bocadillo* for you. No time for breakfast. You like *chorizo*, no? Sorry don Noel. Breakfast in your vehicle. I drive. You eat. Come. *Vamos!*"

As they began to hurry down the stairs Noel Reid suddenly stopped in his tracks.

"*Un momento, señores,*" he said authoritatively. "I'm not going anywhere until you tell me what the devil is going on. And I drive."

Having fought in two World Wars and commanded a battalion in Somalia, he was not one to surrender to a couple of junior police officers, whether they were the feared Spanish lawmen or not.

Normal citizens would not get away with questioning a Guardia Civil policeman and *Sargento* Peréstolo looked as if he had been spat at in the face by a camel in the Spanish Sahara. It was probably the irritation bursting forth after a being on duty all night. Thankfully a nasty situation was averted when the Lieutenant decided there was no harm in offering *el señor inglés* an explanation and allowing him to drive his own vehicle.

"We have orders to take you to Puerto de la Cruz immediately. You drive. I go with you. *El sargento* will follow. We go now. Sorry. No breakfast. You are required to make a citizen's arrest."

Noel Reid's eye suddenly began to show a flicker of enthusiasm.

"*Un criminal inglés,*" added Lieutenant Herrero enticingly.

If only they had told Noel Reid before. His face beamed with delight. This was just his cup of tea. Action. For a man of seventy two he looked and acted like a man in his fifties and he flung his bag into the back of the Land Rover and jumped in behind the wheel. It took an eternity for the old diesel engine to shudder into life but they soon sped along the dusty street out of the town towards the new tarmac, main road to Granadilla.

Behind him and the Lieutenant the grumpy
Guardia, Sergeant Peréstolo struggled to keep
up. He was having a blasphemous and
expletive conversation with himself when the
radio crackled into life.

It was the Granadilla HQ. The suspect had
apparently left Puerto de la Cruz and was now
at Los Rodeos, the airport up on the plateau
close to La Laguna. Today it is called Tenerife
North. In those days it was the island's only
airport.

There was no way Peréstolo could
communicate with the vehicle disappearing
into the distance so he barked at his colleague
in Granadilla to intercept the other Land
Rover as it drove through Granadilla.

"*Que coño pasa ahora?*" swore the Lieutenant
wondering what else could go wrong when
they were waved to a halt by two other men in
uniform in Granadilla.

In Puerto de la Cruz Captain Galvan's
investigations had found that the individual
suspected of being *Napoleon* was staying at a
friend's apartment. But now, that very
morning, he had been seen to leave the
apartment and to hop into a taxi. The taxi had
been followed to the airport.

Whoever this suspected criminal might be, he was about to catch an aeroplane.

From Granadilla the road wound in and out of *barrancos* carved into the yellow, southern landscape by millions of years of torrential, tropical rainstorms. Today a modern motorway now eases one at speed around the island. In the 1960s the old south road needed patience and a long time, twisting and turning and crossing narrow stone bridges. The road took them through the village of Arico, well known for its fruit and wines, and then on to Fasnia.

The calcareous deposit accumulated on the surface of the tufa strata along this part of Tenerife was monotonous and only the *tabaiba dulce*, the Euphorbia balsamifera and other succulents provided any greenery. By mid-morning, when they arrived at the agricultural town of Guimar, the dry landscape had encouraged thirst and they stopped for water and diesel. The man at the petrol pump was in no hurry to pump the pump, especially for men in green. Even Noel Reid began to show signs of impatience. The opportunity of arresting a wanted criminal might be slipping away.

The twisting nature of the road continued

through and beyond the small village of Arafo where new terracing was being prepared for an increasing demand for local tomatoes. Noel Reid was very familiar with the region and, if he hadn't needed to carry out his duty as a British subject, he would happily have stopped off to spend more time with his old tomato-growing friends.

Relief came when the dry southern air suddenly gave way to a cooler, light mist. They were entering the La Laguna plateau, passing the military barracks and the greener fields and stone cottages of Geneto.

So close were they to the Los Rodeos aerodrome that they could hear the roaring engines of an aircraft. Minutes later, as the white walls and red tiles of La Laguna came into view, so did an aircraft.

It was a Lockheed Super Constellation taking off towards the sea. It was one of the last of these exotic flying machines to be used by Spain's Iberia Airlines. The very same aircraft crashed in heavy fog on landing at Los Rodeos two years later.

After a few minutes Noel Reid and his escort entered the pretty white Los Rodeos airport buildings. They ran out into the gardens as far as the hedge which separated the terminal from two parked Dakotas. In the distance the Constellation's silver body flashed in the sunlight before banking slightly into a north easterly direction on its way to Madrid.

Twenty minutes hadn't passed after taking off when a gentleman seated towards the rear of the aircraft ordered his first brandy and soda of the day. He was an Englishman travelling under the name of Mr Kenneth Mills and he spoke to the passenger beside him almost in a whisper. It was a very slight London accent with a Suffolk rounding to it.

Neither Noel Reid not the local authorities in Tenerife ever confirmed whether Mr Shouldham's suspicions had been correct. The idea was simply brushed under a carpet. The maths teacher did bring the matter up frequently in casual conversation. But nobody took him seriously. After all, the man did drink a bit.

It was never admitted nor denied that *Napoleon* or the mastermind behind the Great Train Robbery, Bruce Reynolds, had been to Tenerife. Questions persisted for some months, of course. But the official explanation on the island was that similarities in the name of the passenger travelling to Madrid and Keith Miller, the false name the train robber adopted in his escape to Mexico, had been a coincidence.

UNDER THE WATERFALL

When I was a boy growing up on the Canary Island of Tenerife I spent most of the day with my best friends exploring what was known as the Hanging Hill. We would amuse ourselves by capturing innocent lizards or watching tent-web spiders roll up grasshoppers which we cruelly flung into the maze of their webs.

I would also find immense pleasure helping the men in the banana plantation on the edge of our home or analysing the difference between species of frog. The Iberian water frogs were easy so spot sunbathing on the algae which floated on the great water tanks. The smaller, green Mediterranean tree frog played hide and seek, sheltering in the damp shadows of the banana plants.

Half a century later, not so very long ago, my wife ordered me to go away for a long weekend. She said it would be good to escape the horrors of stress and din of modern life. I must have become impossible and even more bad-tempered than usual because she booked for me to stay at a small country house in what local people know as *the low island*, miles away from any form of distraction.

The remote lowlands lie as far away on the island as one can go, hidden away between the vast cliffs which border the glorious Teno Mountains and the Atlantic Ocean. I discovered, to my delight, that *La Casa Amarilla*, the yellow house to which I was sent on my solitary vacation, was in the middle of a banana plantation and that there was a large water tank close by. It was a paradise for frogs. I felt quite at home.

It was early November and the air was beginning to freshen with the promise of good rains but I could have stayed, reading my book, taking tea and daydreaming on the small verandah, forever. It possessed a rather English-colonial charm. In fact, if it wasn't for the cement buildings of the nearby village of La Caleta de Interián, nestled between the house and the sea, I might have been in an old English colony in the 1950s, somewhere in the tropics. There was certainly evidence of 19th century England with Regency furniture and bookshelves adorned with fine china.

Of course, there has been a relationship between Canary Islanders and the British Isles for centuries, ever since the Spanish islands began to attract merchants looking for good wines and sugar, and when pirates found easy prey in these waters or shadowed ships on their way to the Americas and India. Many British and Irish travellers began to settle in the islands as a result. In fact there's many an aristocratic household in the islands which still boast magnificent pieces of English fine china and antique furniture. However, there was something about La Casa Amarilla that intrigued me. I don't know if it was the large painting of the lady on horseback which dominated the drawing room, the number of frog ornaments on every shelf and table or simply that the house had a certain aura which I can't put into words. I just needed to find out more about it. My questions began at breakfast on the following morning.

Clementina, the same lady who gave me the key to my room when I arrived, served my breakfast. She was the administrator, housekeeper and waitress all in one. She was very kind and patient.

"I noticed the painting in the drawing room is of a lady called María Cólogan. Does the house belong to the Cólogan family?" The origins of the Cólogan dynasty in Tenerife, incidentally, go back to the end of the 17th century when the first of the Irish Colgans arrived on the island.

"No, *señor.* It belongs to *Doña* Teresa Acevedo who restored the house and opened it as the beautiful rural hotel it is today," replied Clementina as she filled a jug with freshly squeezed orange and papaya.

"Do you know who built it and when? Its design and architectural style is not in the normal Canary Island custom," I prompted.

"I've heard people say it was once where an Englishman lived. These fresh croissants are from El Aderno in Buenavista," said Clementina, offering me one from a small basket.

"Really? That *is* interesting. Is there anywhere I can read about the history of the house?" I asked, accepting a croissant.

"I don't think so, Sir. But I have a nephew who works at the town council in Los Silos.

Would you care for some more coffee?"

Before I could delve deeper into her kindness Clementina disappeared into the kitchen. The croissants from *El Aderno*, a legendary bakery, were exceptional and the fig jam was simply delicious with a good hint of lemon juice to give it a special touch.

I forgot all about my intrigue and resumed my anti-stress treatment on the verandah. After a while I perched my reading glasses on a book about Alexander Von Humboldt, the great German naturalist and explorer, and began to enjoy the warmth of the November sun on my face.

My moment of meditation ended when Clementina came up the steps from the drive. The kind lady had come to give me a piece of paper with the name Alejandro scribbled on it. Alejandro was her nephew and the historian at the town council in the old town of Los Silos which was just along the main road. This is so typical of Canary Islanders. Their willingness to be helpful and pride in their unique heritage comes quite naturally. But it was Clementina's turn to ask the questions.

"Do you live in Tenerife, Mr Reid?" she enquired politely, knowing very well that I was not a proper foreigner.

"Yes, as a matter of fact I do. In Puerto."

"*Claro.* I thought so. What is your profession?"

That sudden line of questioning threw me off guard. It didn't seem to be the kind of question a guest would expect from a housekeeper in the low island, or anywhere else for that matter. Loose chatter about the scenery or the weather, or even information about what to do in the neighbourhood would have been appropriate. But I suppose it was my own fault for asking so many questions myself which, to her, may have sounded interfering too.

"I'm an author," I fibbed.

I still don't know what made me say that. It just came out that way. As I say, the question was not expected. I've never been good in exams. Thinking back at the moment, I suppose I wasn't proud of my real, stressful, ordinary job. Pretending to be a writer might have seemed a good excuse at the time for staying on my own at a house in the middle of the banana plantation.

La Casa Amarilla could indeed be the perfect haunt for a temperamental author. It is a place to find solace and tranquillity. It can also provide inspiration in stormy weather.

Carved into the cliff above there is a giant waterfall. It is the final offering of a gorge known as Correa's Leap. Some people call it Espinosa's Escape and, when it rains, the water falls nearly 600 feet. Its roar is like constant thunder. A bodega, Espinosa's Bodega, is just under the waterfall. It only opens during the Saint Andrew's Day festivities on 30th November, when a religious procession leaves the church in La Caleta and carries the sculpture of their patron, Saint Andrew, as far as the small hamlet of houses below the waterfall. It is a tradition for wine and *churros* to welcome the worshippers at the end of their solemn ritual.

□□□□□□□□□

I could easily have spent the whole day reading my book about the invention of nature on that verandah, enjoying the silence and letting all that stress ebb away to the sound of the occasional cricket tuning up its forewings. But I've never been comfortable just sitting. Anyway, the house in the middle of the banana plantation was urging me to peep beyond the bananas. I appeared to have intrigued Clementina too.

Having slipped away again she appeared a few minutes later with an elderly gentleman.

"*Señor*, this is Olegario. He will take you now to see Alejandro."

This was not a suggestion. It was a command, worthy of any senior housekeeper during the course of the day. Therefore, before I had time to make excuses, I was being ushered down the drive to an awaiting vehicle. It was a rusty old white Fiat Panda and it had seen better times running errands on the estate. The torn, red passenger's seat certainly had, as I realised when I sank down into its springs. Olegario had the privilege of a banana-stained, plastic cushion to keep his head above the steering wheel.

"*Va a llover!*" said the old Spaniard, breaking the ice in an obvious way as we drove through the bananas.

He said he knew it was going to rain

because the crickets had begun to chirp during the morning. Olegario informed me that the insects generally rubbed their forewings during the nights when they were courting their mates. If they made their rhythmical sounds in daylight, he assured me, gesticulating with a pair of large, worn hands, it meant rain was on the way. I had no reason not to believe him.

Olegario's was a face wrinkled by time and wisdom. His sharp, blue eyes peeping from beneath a wide straw hat and his interest in nature found in me an eager listener. On the way to Los Silos he told me that he had been a fisherman as well as a workman in the banana plantation and he had time to give another reason for predicting rain by pointing at the sea.

"Look. The sea is as calm as the water in the water tank. It means it is going to rain. Tomorrow the sea will be *rabioso*, in a fury as the storm passes over. The frogs were making a lot of noise last night. Tonight they will be silent as the waterfall thunders."

Before I had time to suggest that meteorologists might consider consulting crickets to help them provide more accurate weather forecasts, Olegario parked the old Fiat in the cobbled street below the old square. The old gentleman pointed me towards the visitor's centre.

"You will find *Alejandrito* in there," said the old fisherman, indicating an ancient building across the square before he disappeared into the bar under the old bandstand kiosk.

The square, La Plaza de la Luz, named after the Virgin of the Light, is an enchanting place and evidently the life and soul of Los Silos. Steeped in history the Virgin adorns the Our Lady of the Light church, and she is venerated by fishermen.

Before going to find Alejandro, I decided to take a look inside the church. Although its origins go back to 1521 the exterior is clearly neo-gothic after it was rebuilt in the early 20th century. A young man standing on the steps leading to the front door revealed his own version of a legend that has enjoyed its twists and turns, as I have since discovered. Nevertheless his story caught my imagination, perhaps because he naturally believed I was a proper foreign tourist. He told me, in almost perfect English, that the Lady of the Light was brought to the island by a Portuguese merchant in the 16th century and that, after being swept to sea in a storm, she had lit up the way for a fishing boat from the Port Orotava. I discovered many things that morning.

I found Alejandro in an office of creaking floorboards after striding up a wooden staircase on the other side of a large Spanish courtyard. I was in the restored 17th century San Sebastian Convent of the Nuns of the Saint Bernard Order, a charming relic which is now used as a tourist office, administrative offices and for exhibitions.

"How lucky you are to work in such an

historical monument," I said, after walking into Alejandro's office uninvited. I had evidently interrupted some serious research but he could not have been more gracious.

"*Buenos días, señor.* I have been expecting you. I understand you are investigating the Englishman who lived in La Casa Amarilla in the 19th century."

"Well, not exactly investigating. Just curious. Was he an Englishman?"

"Oh, yes indeed," he said, "La Casa Amarilla belonged to an Englishman. His name was Jorge Parke French."

"George Parker French?"

"No, no. His name was Jorge Parke French," corrected Alejandro. "But you should go and ask Hernán Fernandez. He will know much more."

Alejandro picked up the telephone and told me he would call the other gentleman.

"There is no reply," he said, putting his hands up and shrugging his shoulders. "Here, I will give you Hernán's telephone number." Alejandro tore off the corner of a page from a newspaper and scribbled down the telephone number of Mr Fernandez.

"Is there anything you can tell me about Mr Jorge Parke?" I asked, using the Spanish pronunciation he preferred.

Alejandro was extremely courteous and kind but I did feel I was interrupting his work and decided not to press too much. I wrote down my email address and handed it to him. Afterwards I realised I must have been acting like a detective in a television series. However, as I turned to leave he added a piece of vital information, as if it was of no importance at all. It was vitally important as far as I was concerned.

"*El inglés* was the founder of the municipal band in 1899. He became very much a part of the community. That is why we call him *Jorge* and not George, as you do in England. The band he formed was called the *La Unión Philharmonic Society*. He was an English guardsman, you know."

I returned to the frogs and my book on the verandah for two more days before settling down again to the routine of ordinary life in the modern world. It rained, just as Olegario and his crickets had promised. It was brief, but hard enough for me to marvel at the thundering waterfall, and I could not let the English guardsman out of my thoughts. So, one morning, three weeks later, I drove down to see Mr Fernandez of Los Silos.

I discovered Hernán, as he insisted I call him, sitting on a kitchen chair on the pavement outside his small town house. It was mid-morning and he was chatting to a woman who was hanging out her washing on the roof of the house opposite. Hernán was a widower and well over eighty but he had a challenging and active mind. Ushering me into his small living room, he teased the neighbour about her husband's very modern underpants which she was hanging on a line lovingly and in very precise formation.

I liked Hernán instantly but got the impression that he was quite suspicious of me. That is, until I told him how much I liked his poetry. You see, he seemed much more interested in reciting his own verses than in my amateurish investigations. I listened and occasionally questioned. But most of the time I listened. He was the elder and I have been reasonably well brought up.

After a while I began to assume that most of his knowledge may not have been knowledge at all, but rumour and supposition, based on years of tales passed from generation to generation. Nevertheless, it was accurate enough to abate my intrigue. After all, it was all I wanted to know and suspected. La Casa

Amarilla had been an Englishman's home in this remote part of the island.

When Hernán presented me with a copy of his own book, which was titled *Mis Vidas Varias*, a compilation of poems and personal experiences, I also realised that Alejandro would be right. Whether factually correct or not, Hernán would know more about the first English resident at the house in the banana plantation than anyone.

As far as Hernán knew, Mr Parke, musician and previously an English guardsman, had been sent to Tenerife as accountant and manager of the Manchester firm of Lathbury and Company whose interests included the Ycod and Daute Estate Company, Ltd., producers of sugar in Tenerife and Gran Canaria. In fact it appeared the company was responsible for one of the last sugarcane plantations on the island and that it was situated in the vicinity of Los Silos and La Caleta de Interián.

The sugarcane was replaced by the bananas which now engulf La Casa Amarilla, her water tanks, her crickets and her frogs. Nevertheless, on the rocky coast, on the east side of the cove below the house, stands a large building with a high chimney. This is the only remaining evidence of a thriving sugar industry. It was once the sugar mill. Today it is used as a banana packing shed, where freshly cut bunches of green bananas are divided into *manillas*, boxed and taken to the markets.

I was about to thank Hernán for receiving me and for his valuable information when he began to recite another poem. I am still not certain whether he was reciting one of his old poems or if he was making up the verse just for my sake. But the words sunk too deep for me to ignore them.

Mr Parke may have been a reasonable accountant and a decent musician, but I deduced from Hernán's verse that the Guardsman had fallen prey to the common temptations of 19th century despotism. The verse suggested the man had made use of his position for carnal satisfaction and that Hernán may have been connected in blood to the Englishman.

"That means you are half English!" Hernán's revelation was astonishing, but I tried to make light of it.

"Yes, Jorge Parke was the father of my father."

"So he married a local girl?" I prompted, attempting innocence.

"No, *muchacho*. He was just my father's father. My grandmother was a young woman working in the plantation."

"Are you saying that your grandfather was the illegitimate child of Jorge Parke?"

"*Sí señor*. Precisely."

I somewhat over-acted an expression of horror.

"Oh, no *hombre*. *Se hacía*. It was done. The daughters of the servants were often taken by the boss. It was done. Those were different times. The Spanish *dueños* were worse."

"Even so. It wasn't right!"

Of course, I knew it happened in those feudal times and well into the 20th century in fact. However, as a fellow countryman of Mr Parke, I wanted to feel shame.

"*Ay mi madre*, but I would not be here had Jorge Parke not taken my grandmother for his lover, *eh?*" joked Hernán.

"Anyway, he was not a bad man. He was a good man. Who knows? Perhaps it was she who took him."

Hernán could see me struggling to digest the philosophy and was kind enough to break my silence.

"Did you know there is a rock pool named after Jorge Parke?"

Indeed there is a rock pool in La Caleta known as *Charco El Inglés*, the Englishman's pool. It is a natural pool shaped into the volcanic bay known as La Caleta de Interián. It is named after the Englishman who frequently took a dip in it. What I didn't know was that the Englishman was the same Mr Parke who lived in the yellow house.

Hernán finally convinced me. Not so much that his illegitimate English grandfather may have been a bit of rogue of sorts, as well as the founder of the municipal band at Los Silos. Hernán convinced me that Jorge Parke must have been an eccentric character and therefore possibly colourful and attractive to women. As I walked up the lane towards my car Hernán recited a final verse to his revealing poem.

Stained with love
Sweet sugar and rum
A camel he rode
To bathe in salty cove

□□□□□□□□□

On my way to the car I felt thirsty and hungry and paused at the bar under the bandstand at the square. The Plaza de La Luz was radiant with early preparations for the Christmas festivities. A stage was being created for the nativity scene at Nazareth. The new-born Jesus would soon attract the three wise Kings of Orient on their desert camels.

With visions of Mr Parke riding another camel down to the rock pool fading rapidly I sat down under the shade of one of the magnificent Indian laurels and ordered a cool beer, a board of goat cheese and some *fabada*.

Almost immediately a familiar voice interrupted my thoughts.

"Did he tell you about the waterfall?"

It was my old friend, Olegario. We were pleased to see each other again. I smiled to myself, however. How old-fashioned of these people to know what everyone was up to. The word of mouth telegraph had been up and down the lanes of Los Silos announcing my visit to Hernán, the poet.

"No, he did not. What about the waterfall?"

"*No era tan malo*." Olegario also defended the English guardsman, attempting to assure me that Parke was not such a bad sort at all.

I was about to be indiscreet by asking the old fisherman if he too was related in blood to Jorge Parke when he continued with his own explanation.

"*Que va!* A man who plays music can never be bad. No, it was the other man. His colleague was the bad one."

"His colleague? Oh, I am sorry. Here, please sit down. Join me for lunch." I sensed there was another snippet of vital information about to be revealed and pulled up a chair, urging him to sit.

"*Bueno*, perhaps *un vinito*. It's early for lunch. It's never too early for a cup of wine. Yes, there was another man working with him," continued Olegario as he sat down.

"You are going to tell me something about

the waterfall? I saw it the other day. The spray reached La Caleta."

"Yes, when it falls, it falls."

"Was there another man? Did Jorge Parke have a friend?"

"Yes. I remember my father telling me about another foreigner who worked with *el señor Parke* and that the man was worse than the devil."

"Was he English too?"

"I don't know. He was not from here, of course. But where he came from I do not know. My father heard the story from his father. From what I remember the man worked for Jorge Parke but he was lazy and drank and was cruel to the people in the plantation. *Lo echaron*. They kicked him out. Others say *el hombre* ran away after he found the box under the waterfall."

My beer was losing its chill and the *fabada* remained untouched. Hunger had given way to intrigue once again. I've never liked roundabout explanations but I knew patience would bring its rewards.

"What box under the waterfall? Is the wine good? Would you like another cup?" I offered, begging him to want another, needing Olegario to tell me about the mysterious box that had found its way into the tale.

"*Bueno*, it's neither very, very good nor very, very bad. It's what there is. It keeps the devil away and the mechanical parts greased," he said, referring to the red wine of course.

"Now I remember. They called the man *el cornudo*."

"Who?"

"The other man. El Cornudo. He possessed ginger eyebrows as big as horns, the man who worked for Jorge Parke," said Olegario, swallowing a second cup of wine.

As I know today, a person who is *cornudo* can either mean that the unfortunate man was cuckolded or, as in this particular case, according to Olegario, that he was horned by those giant, ginger eyebrows. I remember joining Olegario with the next quarter of wine after my beer had become warm. I ordered another helping of *fabada*, a delicious bean and pork stew and Olegario accepted my invitation when it was time for a *canario* to lunch. Early afternoon began to turn into evening and numerous cups of wine helped grease not only the memory and the mechanical parts, but also the imagination. Olegario's story ebbed and flowed. Whether it was true or not, he brought back memories of my father who would tell me tales of pirates and contraband in the Canary Islands.

The islands' waters were riddled with pirates and corsairs, Father would say, from Frenchman, Jambe de Bois and John Hawkins to the Barbary pirates. His favourite stories, which would have me awake long after bedtime, were about two Canary Islanders. One was the elegant corsair, Amaro Pargo about whom so much has been written in recent years. The other was the unfortunately named *Cabeza de Perro*. He was known as Dog Head on account of his ugly face and deformed head. Legend suggests he was born in a tiny, stone cottage on the slopes above Igueste de San Andrés, near the port of Santa Cruz, but that he went on to own a palace in Havana. My father told me it was filled with gold-framed mirrors. I think the idea gave me nightmares. How could anyone so deformed want to collect mirrors?

"*Cabeza de Perro* frequently sailed back to the Canary Islands," continued Olegario. "They said he would follow English ships across the Atlantic and then attack them when they were heavy with gold."

"Yes, but surely the activity of pirates ended long before Jorge Parke and his colleague were in the sugarcane plantations," I interrupted.

"*Hombre*, of course! It must have been in the previous century at least, although there have been many stories about the activity of pirates in the 19th century too and," he whispered, signalling with his eyes in the direction of the town hall, "there are pirates of another kind today."

We laughed out loud. Olegario was a good raconteur. I decided not to question his information again, although it occurred to me that the old man must have sat on the verandah of the Casa Amarilla many a time. Perhaps he had allowed the banana leaves, fluttering in the sea breeze, to stir his imagination too, but I wanted to know what box had entered the story and whether it had anything to do with La Casa Amarilla.

I listened to his story unfurling with the wine. In his brigantine's cabin, *Cabeza de Perro* kept a chest full of silver and pearls. He resorted to these when bribing negotiators and fellow scoundrels. Once, lying in wait for a victim, the pirate feared he had been betrayed after doing some business with a gentleman in Tenerife. Believing his ship would be inspected he weighed anchor and sailed round the island to position the ship off La Caleta de Interián. He and a member of his gang rowed ashore with the chest.

"Waiting for them was the priest from the town of Buenavista. The priest and the brigand were childhood friends in Igueste," explained Olegario.

The understanding was that, if anything should happen to the pirate, the contents of the chest would go to the poor of Igueste, with the church as trustee. However, the chest should be kept close to *La Caleta* in a secret hideaway until further notice. The place chosen was a cave just to the west of the waterfall, near enough but difficult for anyone to reach or to come across by chance.

That waterfall again, I thought to myself.

As I suspected, Dog Head never returned to La Caleta. The priest from Buenavista also disappeared soon after assisting the pirate. Some people said he went to join the pirate in his pillaging on the high seas. Others believed *Cabeza de Perro* did not trust his old friend and either murdered the unfortunate collaborator or abducted him back to the ship.

"One or two people reckon that on that same night the pirate had also taken time to pillage silver from the church of Buenavista, as well as a small, wooden sculpture of Jesus.

"They said the little statue was to keep the pirate's ship safe from you English!" teased Olegario, with signs that the red, local wine had greased more than was needed.

It seems the next time Cabeza de Perro returned to the island of Tenerife he was disguised as an honest citizen in clean, white clothes. Unfortunately for him, his luck had run out. He never made it back to La Caleta. The man they called Dog Head was easily recognised, arrested and executed in Santa Cruz.

"What happened to the chest? Did anyone ever find Dog Head's silver?" I asked, rather mockingly I'm afraid, as I had begun to doubt every word again.

"I don't know. *Hombre*, what is certain is that *Cabeza de Perro* would not have found his silver or his pearls anyway."

"Oh? So someone else did find the chest? Was there really a chest in that cave?" I suddenly began to believe again.

"Who knows? But my father said his father suspected the colleague of Jorge Parker heard the same story about the box and that he went to search under the waterfall."

"So it might have been true then? The

friend of Jorge Parke, the bad man they called *el cornudo* disappeared after finding the treasure?"

"No. Not at all. You see there was no silver. There were no pearls," replied Olegario shrugging his shoulders. His bottom lip ejected out as if to enforce the mystery.

"Well, I am pleased to hear it. It served *el cornudo* right. He got what he deserved for his greed and brutality," I said. It must have been the wine or the story teller, but I truly fell for the tale again.

"*Bueno*, that is what it would seem."

"So, the chest was empty. If there were ever any silver and pearls, who do you think took them, Olegario?"

"*El cura*, of course! Who else?"

"What?"

"*Si señor*. What you are hearing. My grandfather swore it was the priest. He believed the priest from Buenavista disappeared after keeping the treasure for himself."

"I don't believe it! But why? What made your grandfather suggest that?"

"Well, because of what *el cornudo* found in the box under the waterfall."

"Do mean to tell me there was something

else in the chest?"

"Indeed there was, and this is why my grandfather believed the priest had taken the silver and pearls for himself. The box was not empty. The silver and pearls had been removed, yes, but there was something much more valuable in their place. *El cornudo* got the reward he deserved. Instead of eternal wealth he found the eternal spirit. Inside the box was the wooden Jesus stolen from the church in Buenavista."

INNOCENT SCOUNDREL

Reaching the top of the gangway they both looked over their shoulders to see what all the commotion was about. London's Victoria Dock was still, in 1960, an oily hive of activity, but a loud-voiced woman wearing a pink hat under which she could not be seen from above, was shrieking alarmingly at a lanky man following her with luggage. The mechanical din of the shipping industry could not compete with her.

"Poor man! I do hope their cabin isn't next to ours," said Janet Turnbull.

She and her husband Ted were on their way back to the Canary Islands after an intense couple of weeks visiting family and promoting the island of Tenerife as a retirement destination. Ted, as everyone knew him, had semi-retired to Tenerife in 1957 after selling his highly prized farm in Sussex. An accident with a tractor left him with a leg injury and, unable to enjoy the farm as he had since he was a boy, he called it a day. But he was still only forty two and always on the lookout for a business opportunity. He found one in Tenerife. He realised early on that there was potential for selling properties to a new generation of affluent British travellers and second-home owners.

Janet, who was twelve years younger than Ted, had taken to the Canary Islanders easily and they adored her. Life and the temperate climate had become idyllic. Their eldest boy had already started prep school in England and their second, still only eight, would soon follow.

Ted had always been drawn to the Orotava Valley and Puerto de la Cruz. Many years prior to settling in Tenerife, a great uncle of his owned the Turnbull Hotel. It had been just up the cobbled street from the fishing port and one of the first British boarding houses to offer rooms to travellers towards the end of the nineteenth century.

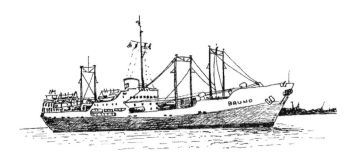

On this occasion the Turnbulls had booked a cabin aboard the Bruno, a fruit ship belonging to the Norwegian Fred Olsen Line. Launched in 1948 the Bruno was specifically constructed to transport bananas and other goods from the Canary Islands to London where the fruit would end up in markets like Covent Garden. Like her sister ship, the Bencomo, they were regular visitors to the ports of Santa Cruz and Las Palmas and also carried passengers.

Only minutes had passed when a silver-haired tower of a Viking knocked gently on their cabin door and asked if they would like a cup of tea whilst they unpacked. It was their steward, Morten. He would be Janet's saviour on more than one occasion throughout the voyage.

No, he informed them, the lady with the large, pink hat would be travelling in a single cabin on the port side.

"That's a blessing. I wonder who the poor man with her baggage was." Janet waited for their steward to depart before making that comment, of course, and then peered out of their porthole across the water towards Canning Town.

"Oh dear! Darling, I think I've got to lie down for a bit. I'll unpack later. I'm beginning to feel seasick."

"You can't possibly be feeling sick already," barked Ted. "We are still tied up and she doesn't sail for an hour or two. Come on, let's go on deck and watch them load the holds."

As anyone knows, the beginnings of voyage can often imply a spell of nausea until sea legs have taken over. One can understand how Mrs Turnbull felt but it wasn't, of course, the movement of the ship upon the swell. As her husband rightly pointed out, the Bruno was firmly tied to the shore on a pond of still water. It was more likely the oily smells of the port, the shouted dialect of the stevedore and, quite possibly, some imagination.

Nevertheless, Janet's throat was dry and her hands began to feel clammy. At one moment she felt hot and in another she felt a chill. There was that all too familiar feeling churning in her stomach as she followed her husband along the passageway and out onto the deck.

"There you are, you see," he encouraged. "We are still alongside. It only proves what I have always said. Your feeling seasick is purely imagination"

"Probably," replied Janet rather feebly.

"It is. It's your imagination. You are imagining the worst when the ship is motionless on a duck pond!"

"I'm not imagining! I'm anticipating!"

"Well, stop anticipating! Come on. Let's walk up to the bows and get some air. You'll be fine in a minute and we'll order some champagne as we sail down the Thames!"

Her husband was always cheerful! He would be cheerful even if the Bruno was sinking, but the thought of champagne made Janet feel anything but cheerful. She felt as if she were turning green and collapsed onto a deckchair.

"Just leave me here. You go and look around. I just want to sit here and die for a while!"

Ted knew the signs. He had been there before. His pretty little wife was always a bundle of fun and he loved her more than anything in the world, but the moment she stepped on a ship she became another person. Ted knew he should have been unselfish and got them a flight on one of the new British United Airways Viscounts. He bent over to kiss her cheek and marched off to explore. Janet closed her eyes.

The moment of peace and self-pity lasted less than it took her husband to walk the length of the deck.

"Feeling a teeny-weeny bit queasy, are we?" said the high-pitched soprano voice.

"Already, my dear?" it queried annoyingly.

Janet opened her eyes. What she saw was that pink hat. More than a hat, it was almost as wide as an umbrella and it had tiny purple pansies decorating the rim. The face peering down at her was in its mid-forties and the eyes green and teasing. It was certainly attractive, and reminded Janet of a character in a play they had been to see in the West End. Her immediate impression, however, was that the face belonged to one of those creatures men find themselves in a tangle with before they realise that they have been entangled. This woman was a man-eater.

"No, I'm quite alright, thank you."

"You look dreadful, dearie. Your face is green!" said the woman with the pink hat rather mercilessly.

"You're seasick. Horrible, isn't it? I hope I'm not going to be seasick too!"

It must have been intimidating to be faced with this verbal assault at close quarters. All Janet needed was to be left quite alone. But one assumes the new friend was just trying to be kind.

"The best trick is to have a brandy and soda. I'll go and get you one. You'll feel so much better immediately! Oh, and do what I do. Tighten your corset. Do you have a corset?"

"No! Actually I'll be quite alright in a moment. Thank you. It's the smell of diesel mixed with salt water. It always makes me feel odd. Ah, here's my husband," said Janet. She felt relief all of a sudden.

Ted Turnbull was marching back from the bow. He stiffened visibly at the sight of the woman standing so close to his beloved little wife.

The woman with the pink hat had a name. It was Amanda.

"Hello. I'm Amanda. Amanda Lovejoy," she said with an outstretched hand and green eyes hoping to dazzle.

"I'll just go and get those brandy and sodas,

darling," she added, returning her attention to the innocent Mrs Turnbull.

"No. It's quite alright. Edward and I were just going to have a cup of tea, weren't we, Edward? I must unpack, too. But thank you. Thank you so much," said Janet, standing up and making politely sure the woman understood that she was being dismissed.

"But do try the brandy!" she insisted. "I know where you are. You're in the cabin directly opposite mine. I'll pop round later."

There was no chance of that happening, of course, thought Janet. Ted was instantly suspicious of anyone, especially of a woman who showed signs of interfering in a domestic issue. He glared at Mrs Lovejoy as she pranced away down the deck. There was no doubt. However green and hypnotising those eyes he was not that kind of man. His body language was that of a dog having just seen a cat which it especially loathes.

Janet Turnbull remained in her cabin for three days. In fact, she only felt able to join the other group of twelve passengers aboard the cargo ship for the fun and games of a sea voyage after the Bruno had cleared the Bay of Biscay.

Morten, the steward, was most kind

although the good Norwegian kept telling Janet that she should eat as much as she could and he brought her tray after tray of soups, biscuits, toast and pate.

Oddly enough, and much to Ted Turnbull's annoyance, it was Amanda whose company Janet began to tolerate first as the ship churned her stomach southwards. She did indeed *pop in* forever. Although Janet hardly registered her presence for the first couple of days when the going was rough even for those with sea legs, she began to appreciate the woman, as perhaps only a woman could.

Amanda Lovejoy was lonely. She was a widow and had, until her husband died, spent some happy, childless years in Little Marlow, a village in Buckinghamshire. She had moved to London where a relative found her an editing job for the BBC. It paid well and she rented a riverside flat in Barnes.

Janet was conscious enough when Amanda admitted to having had numerous affairs.

"But men are such cowards! I need to get away from one of them."

"To Spain? The Canary Islands are Spanish, you know," Janet said, sounding innocent but knowing perfectly well what she wanted to imply.

"I just want a change. I hear there are some delicious black sand beaches and I intend to spend every hour of sunlight burning myself."

"Well, yes. Of course you do. But do be careful, Amanda!"

"Darling, do you want to see the selection of oils I have brought? I'll hire a parasol too, so don't worry. I want to turn chestnut, not red like a lobster!"

"I'm sure you'll find it very relaxing."

Evidently Janet had tried to be subtle in her efforts to warn the woman in the pink hat about other dangers. Whether Amanda was also disguising her real understanding or not, Janet decided not to become involved further. But Latin men, however elegant and charming, did have a certain reputation.

A thought made Janet smile for the first time on the voyage and offered hope that she was almost ready to stand up and walk the deck. Would Amanda fall for their boundless charms or would the Canary Island men be eaten alive? If Amanda Lovejoy was serious about getting away from men, the Bruno was travelling in the wrong direction.

It was when Amanda kindly offered to look after her husband that Janet suddenly found her sea legs. As a result, Mrs Lovejoy ceased popping in to the Turnbull's cabin and turned her attention to other attractions, unsurprisingly of the male variety. So much for the sessions of psychiatry with Janet Turnbull!

Among the passengers there was a delightful young Spaniard from Santa Cruz, a young honeymoon couple who spent the entire voyage holding hands and an ageing Colonel who had evidently spent much of his career in India. Together with Mr and Mrs Turnbull, they all had the honour of sitting at the Captain's table.

As Janet soon discovered, they had all begun to refer to Mrs Amanda Lovejoy as *that woman*.

It was to be expected. She drove the honeymoon couple to desperation by just talking to them. Amanda discovered that the Spaniard had stomach ulcers and made them worse by pursuing him with different remedies, including brandy. By the third day of the voyage the Colonel, who had apparently fallen instantly for the green eyes, became irritable and resentful and took it out on the quietly spoken Norwegian captain. Mrs Lovejoy had turned her attentions to the Captain after discovering that the poor Colonel was just that, penniless except when ordering another whisky.

Janet concluded that the Captain may have become quietly spoken as a result of having to share his table with that Lovejoy woman.

Nevertheless it was in her nature to be kind and often so seemingly innocent that she actually felt sorry for the pink-hatted woman. After all, the green eyed friend had opened up to her in the confessionary of her cabin. *That woman*, however tiresome and rude, needed to be the centre of attention. Janet put it all down to loneliness.

But Mrs Lovejoy had the unnerving habit of constantly trying to provoke, whether intentionally or not.

"Why do Norwegians always drink so heavily?" she asked the Captain on the fourth evening, just after crossing the Bay of Biscay. Even kind Janet was confused by that outburst, especially as the Bruno's captain drank nothing but milk.

"I don't know. Do we?" replied the Captain.

"Oh, yes. Always. They are quite unlike our own British sailors who are so well behaved and respected around the world. Aren't they, Colonel?"

The Colonel mumbled something to Ted

Turnbull. It was the wrong question to ask the Army man. The old Colonel had never trusted anyone in the Navy, especially after a team from a British frigate had beaten his team of Sikhs in a football match during a shore visit in India.

"I'm told Latin men are incredibly passionate!" said Amanda, turning her attention to the young Spaniard while Janet Turnbull nearly choked into her serviette.

□□□□□□□□□

After six days at sea the Bruno was nudged alongside the south mole in Santa Cruz. The port was buzzing with activity and ships of all shapes and sizes were unloading and loading. The mole was stacked with endless boxes of Canary Island bananas. One or two black Peugeot and Mercedes taxis with their familiar red stripes down their sides and green sunshades hung around hoping for custom in between banana lorries. Everyone shouted at everyone else.

"It's so nice to be home, darling!" said Janet Turnbull as they walked towards the dark blue Rover where Eusebio, the chauffeur, was waiting. As they drove away the woman with the pink hat was seen negotiating with a gesticulating taxi driver.

Amanda Lovejoy didn't like what she saw during that taxi ride. Vehicles screeched around the bends, hooting at everything. The driver's left arm hung limp out of the window whilst he changed gear and thumbed the steering wheel in the right direction with the other. Skeletal dogs wandered aimlessly towards their death at the roadsides and, later on, she couldn't bear the sight of those birds imprisoned in tiny cages at the front of almost every little house they passed on their way to the Orotava Valley. There was fog as they drove past the airport and a dense cloud hung over Puerto de la Cruz. Not a sign of the famous volcano.

Her stomach had shrunk at the dreariness of the roadside. Like many a tourist, she was bluffed by her first impression and in her disappointment could not imagine the significance of the little green and brown fields, the volcanic, stone walls, the vineyards or the terracing on the edges of the deep *barrancos* which had been carved into the land by thousands of years of winter rainstorms. The shadows under the little stone bridges, the barns, the wooden carts, the thatched cottages and the water troughs meant little to a solitary, sun-seeking woman from England. She knew nothing of the island people, of how they had toiled to make rocks gush with mountain water for their crops and livestock or how they had performed miracles, blessed by ancient wines, to plant fields where there was once volcanic debris. She had not yet felt their gentle passion. It didn't dawn on her that in fact she had arrived on a land blessed by the Gods, one of the *fortunate islands* of Macaronesia.

Mrs Lovejoy's first impression of the island's only tourist resort in the early 1960s was equally disappointing. There were a couple of black sand beaches to roast upon, of course, and rock pools and a colourful fishing port and plaza. But there were no casinos or Mediterranean bars open all night. It was all too peaceful and quiet for her until she moved to a new hotel on the seafront called the Las Vegas and discovered the San Telmo lido. The facilities included two modern swimming pools and a bar which closed at midnight. The bar was where anyone who was anyone, or who wanted to be anyone, went to after dark.

It was also at the San Telmo lido that she made a local friend. The expression *picked up* might sound crude but would probably be correct. However, who picked up whom would be a matter of interpretation, for the local gentleman in question was a man called Inocente.

He was one of those freelancers one would meet every day on every street corner, smoking a cigarette at the bar in the plaza or, more recently, hanging around the lido bar hoping to accept an invitation to become a handsome escort.

His favourite occupation during daylight hours was to comb the sands and seaside avenue for a lonely foreigner, often a slightly bewildered lady who would invariably fall for his irresistible Spanish charm.

That might suggest he was an idle swindler. Inocente was anything but idle. He was not well-off and lived day to day from tips and rewards. He won his life, as they say in Spain, by doing anything which needed doing, from running an errand to painting a house or playing with spare children.

□□□□□□□□□

"Mummy, isn't that Inocente?"

It was Janet's youngest son, Jeremy, and he was pointing across the sand towards the cliff end of the Martiánez beach.

It certainly was him! And he was oiling the shoulders of a foreign woman!

"Don't point, darling. It's rude!" she replied.

"Why don't you go and see if Candido will play with you?"

Candido was an urchin, a fisherman's son

Jeremy, or *Yeremi* as the locals knew him, would spend hours with investigating in the rock pools.

But Jeremy had ruined one of his mother's moments of bliss enjoying a good read before others began crowding the afternoon beach. It wasn't that he had interrupted her or that Inocente happened to be on the beach oiling a foreigner. She was quite used to that.

No! It was the pink hat. He was oiling Amanda Lovejoy! Worse still, Janet had been caught peeking! In an instant, Inocente was brushed aside and Amanda was on her feet waving the pink hat at Janet who had no option but to acknowledge the wave, albeit unwillingly.

Amanda looked supremely happy as she approached, towing the innocent behind her. Her swimsuit looked just as happy as the huge pink hat and might have been described as a fruit salad. The Lovejoy woman looked as no woman ever believes she really looks. In other words, abominable.

"*Daaaarling!* How absolutely delicious to find you!" she screeched.

"Good afternoon, Amanda." By Janet's usual, generous standards hers was not an inviting response.

"*Buenos días,* Inocente!" she continued, rather glaring at the Spaniard.

"*Señora,*" he said, looking sideways like a little boy caught red-handed.

"Oh, do you know *Pepe*? He is just divine, isn't he?" she beamed.

Amanda rattled on as Mrs Turnbull again glared at the innocent. Pepe was his professional beach prowler's name. As was his custom he had adopted it for the occasion.

"Pepe is so sweet! We met last night outside the lido and this morning he pointed out his family's estate while he showed me the valley in a car I have hired. All those bananas!"

Janet glared at Inocente again. How did he manage to be so guilty and ooze such charm at the same time? Amanda's *Pepe* was not the owner of a banana plantation. Quite the contrary. In fact he came from a very poor household and his home was just one room divided by a curtain.

"Pepe has offered to be my guide everywhere. Isn't that just wonderful darling?"

Mrs Turnbull's felt her blood beginning to boil and was tempted to challenge Inocente on behalf of the foolish, irritating English woman. She thought about warning Amanda but then she reminded herself that women seldom accept another woman's opinion about a man.

Then, with a certain amount of relief, her blood cooled when she recalled the first impression she had of Amanda Lovejoy aboard the Bruno. She was, after all, a man-eater. Perhaps Inocente was simply allowing himself to be led astray by the not so innocent tourist.

The winter season on the island of Tenerife in the 1960s had begun to bring boat and planeloads of tourists. Puerto de la Cruz had originally become a health resort in the nineteenth century as a result of so many wealthy and adventurous European travellers, artists, geologists and doctors describing the Orotava Valley as a temperate paradise. It was now the destination for early package tourism.

Although residents, especially long established foreigners and Britons of glorious Victorian sentiment lamented the arrival of newcomers and especially of those many began to refer to as *nouveau riche* classes, the coming and going of a new breed of traveller brought its benefits.

The shops were humming with new-found optimism, selling anything from embroidery and fans to castanets. The profession of taxi driver suddenly became more important than the never-smiling bank clerk, and hairdressers were blossoming with the young elite and beautiful, all wanting to look like Natalie Wood. Even those Victorian pillars of the British community, church, club and library were revived by the invasion of the masses. They were days of plenty.

□□□□□□□□□

It was the end of October and that day on the beach was the last for almost two weeks. Right on schedule, the first autumn rains arrived with a vengeance in the Canary Islands and Janet lost touch with Amanda Lovejoy.

The rain kept everyone indoors. The islanders sheltered either in grand houses wallowing in the comfort of French and English furniture, or in their damp and poverty-scented *casa terrera*. The idle on street corners and in the bars were showered away from one of their favourite pastimes, which was to look on at the *extranjeros*.

The torrential rain storms gave way to the *land of eternal spring*, as travel brochures advertised, and the sun began to prickle the pale European skins once again. Mount Teide wore an early coat of snow and for a couple of days brown waters around the coast betrayed signs of torrents having poured down the deep *barrancos*. Very soon the beach begun to flutter again with parasols and tourists eager to burn themselves for a glorious Indian tan.

Janet Turnbull took Jeremy down to the rock pools under the San Telmo chapel. The waves were still too strong on the Martiánez beach and the boy was soon crab-hunting and submerging himself with Candido to chase young, silver mullet in the transparent waters of the big pool.

Janet put her towel down on the stone bench at the end of the small pier and settled down to her book. An old fisherman cast his line out into the deeper waters to her left while tourists mingled with local women selling embroidery and strelitzia on the San Telmo promenade above.

Tenerife was indeed one of the fortunate islands and Puerto de la Cruz was a corner of paradise. The low-tide waves invading the pools and the distant hum of the street combined into a hypnotic effect. The feeling of peace and contentment made Janet close her eyes and enjoy the warmth on her face as the sun peeped through again.

"*Daaaarling!*"

It was that voice again and it pierced into Janet's moment of meditation as if a giant wave had crashed over the pier.

"Fucking hell!"

Janet had completely forgotten about the woman with the pink hat over the last couple of wet weeks and her soprano greeting startled her to such an extent that she lost her usual polite self-control.

The wife of respectable Mr Turnbull glanced around anxiously. She hadn't used that kind of language since her school days playing lacrosse at St Swithun's School and prayed Jeremy had not been within hearing distance. No he hadn't. Even so, he would not have been offended. He and his friend looked much more interested in dissecting an echinoderm, better known as a sea urchin.

Janet then bent her head around Amanda Lovejoy's hat to make certain the only thing the old fisherman cared about was a bobbing float.

Only when she was absolutely certain that nobody had heard did Janet gather herself up and manage a smile. She almost felt as ridiculous as the eccentric English tourist standing in front of her on the small pier.

"Oh, darling! I made you jump, didn't I?

That voice echoed once again across the water and back.

"Sweetie, I'm so sorry, but I spotted you from up there and I just *had* to say goodbye," explained Amanda, pointing up at the promenade.

"You see, my ship sails tonight and you've been so very kind!"

"Not at all. That's very sweet of you. Here, sit down," said Janet patting the stone beside her rather guiltily.

"I mustn't stay darling, thank you. I'm leaving for the port in an hour and I've got to find Pepe before I go. It's terribly important."

"Oh?"

Knowing very well that Amanda was referring to Inocente Janet was not particularly helpful.

"He could be anywhere. Have you tried the *Dinámico* on the plaza?"

"No, but I have to explain something to him. I can't leave Tenerife without clearing a matter up. Something simply awful happened, darling."

Janet looked down at the palms of her hands, letting her feminine intuition take full responsibility of her thoughts.

"Oh?"

"Pepe took me to a place he called *Los Christians*, or something like that. It was pouring with rain here and he promised it would be sunny over the hills on the other side of the island."

"Yes, that often happens. It can be horrible weather on this side and lovely just over the ridge on the south side" said Janet, almost defending the scoundrel.

"Pepe said he knew of somewhere we could stay."

"Go on," Janet encouraged, at the same time trying not to let her imagination run wild at the thought of this not so innocent English woman permitting herself to be led astray by a scoundrel she insisted upon calling *Pepe*.

Los Cristianos was a sleepy fishing village and port for local produce in the early 1960s. It had a fine, yellow-sand beach and was becoming popular amongst wealthy local families from the north of the island. By the end of the 1970s, however, it had fast turned into the beginnings of the island's giant tourist resorts which would one day be a favourite holiday destination for millions of sun-worshipping Europeans.

If the rains were coming in from the north, the south of Tenerife would have been cloudless, a phenomenon only the high mountains and geographers understood.

"It was marvellous, darling. Unfortunately, something simply horrendous happened."

Janet's thoughts ran wilder and wilder as she let her evidently not-so-innocent imagination conjure up all sorts of unheard of forms of love making in the barren landscapes of the south or in the gently lapping waves of Los Cristianos.

"We were only there for two days. You should go there. There is such a lovely beach and the fishing boats tied up in the bay make for a perfect watercolour. I do wish I'd taken a sketchbook."

"Yes, I suppose it would. There is a guest house in Los Cristianos. Did you stay there?" Janet prompted, a little less imaginatively.

"No. We stayed the night in a tiny little house next to the beach. Pepe told me it belonged to an employee of his. It was very quaint, but a bit too simple, I must say. Do you know I'm beginning to think Pepe isn't as wealthy as he makes out he is."

"Oh, dear"

"Anyway darling, I've made a dreadful mistake."

"*Yeees*," replied Mrs Turnbull, once again

studying the palms of her hands.

"Pepe was nowhere to be seen when I woke in the morning so I started to pack my bag. I still hadn't finished packing the two or three things I had taken and a towel when he came back and I began screaming at him."

"Why? What on earth did he do?" asked Janet whose mental creativity had once again been plunged deeply away from innocent thoughts.

"My necklace! My beautiful pearl necklace! I couldn't find it. I accused him of stealing it. Well, when he took me to eat fish the night before he asked me if it was worth a lot of money. What else could I think?"

"I see," said Janet, beginning to suspect Inocente had gone far too far on this occasion.

"He gave me so much wine to drink too. I hardly remembered where I was in the morning. But no one else had been near me in the house. Well, except a friend of his. They talked to for hours, smoking their cigarettes outside in the doorway during the night. What do men find to talk about in the middle of the night?

"At least he had the decency to bring me back to Puerto!"

"Do you want me to take you to the

consulate to report the matter?" Janet asked solemnly, still not daring to inform Amanda Lovejoy that the culprit was in fact called "Innocent."

"Oh no, no, no, no!" screeched Amanda.

"That's just it! Pepe hadn't stolen my necklace at all! Here it is," she said, pulling what was indeed an expensive-looking piece of jewellery from her handbag.

"Oh Lord! Poor Inocente!"

Suddenly Janet Turnbull found pity for the man she had been about to denounce.

"I had tucked the necklace into a stocking in the bottom of my bag. It wasn't until last night when I began preparing my luggage that I discovered it.

"I've made such a beastly mistake" squeaked Amanda, half sobbing.

"I think I should give the necklace to *Pepe*. It's the least I can do, don't you think?"

"I'm not sure that would be a good idea, Amanda," warned Janet. "After all, he would only sell it and spend it on drink and cigarettes."

Amanda at last thought she could speak about the man as he was, just a poor, innocent scoundrel.

"But I must tell him how sorry I am. I

must. I must. Will you tell him if I don't see him? And tell him what a wonderful person he is," she begged.

"Look, Amanda. I think you had better know that Pepe is in fact...."

Before Janet could say any more, Jeremy came between them with a dripping creature from the depths of the rock pools.

"Look Mummy. Look what I've caught!"

He held out his hands to reveal an octopus, with tentacles dangling between fingers. By the look of horror on Amanda Lovejoy's face she had never been as close to a creature of the sea. She had probably never been as close to an adventurous little boy either. But Jeremy had introduced an element of nature into a troubled scene and for once in her life Janet didn't tell her son off for interrupting a conversation between grown-ups.

"Wonderful! Well done, Jeremy! Will you take it back for Carmen to cook or are you going to put it back in the rock pools?"

"Mummy!"

What a thing to suggest. How typically unobservant of his mother. She had never seriously taken an interest in pond-life. Jeremy was a promising naturalist and would never hurt a young creature.

The octopus suddenly stirred and, like a wrestler, its tentacles rapidly did their best to entangle one of her son's hands and arm. Perhaps it was a female octopus. Jeremy began to skip back to the pools and then called over his shoulder.

"Look, Mummy. Here comes Inocente!"

Indeed he was and he was walking towards them along the pier.

"Amanda, you can tell him yourself. Here comes your *Pepe*."

The innocent scoundrel flashed a mischievous white smile at Janet and took off his small straw hat to greet his English friend.

"*Hola* Amanda," he said cheerfully. "*Te estaba buscando!* I was looking for you!"

"I'm so sorry. I beg you, please. I really am

so sorry," said Amanda.

"No. No! *I sorry!* You lost *perlas*. I go to Los Cristianos again. I found nothing. *Nada. Lo siento mucho, amor mío.*"

Janet Turnbull began to pick up her things. She didn't want to become involved. In fact she was feeling most confused. This was not the plot she had anticipated. Was this really the irritating, man-eating woman she had encountered on the Bruno? Had she really discovered something truly adorable in this beach-roaming predator? Was it possible that Inocente actually felt something for the woman with the pink hat? Was that genuine emotion in his voice? Or was it just a magnificent actor being as charmingly cunning as ever?

But she remained for the final act. Janet couldn't abandon now, not being a woman, not after Inocente brought out a small, brown paper parcel from behind his back.

"Is for you, *mi amorcito*," he said handing the parcel to Amanda.

"It is nothing. *Poco dinero*. You like, yes?"

Amanda looked sideways at Janet, took the parcel in her hands and began to untie the string around the paper. Inside was a plain, gentleman's handkerchief, folded double and slightly stained. Amanda looked into Inocente's black eyes. A hint of a tear sparkled like the tip of a wave behind him and he beckoned with his hands for her to carry on.

She unravelled the handkerchief slowly to reveal a string of pearls. A necklace. Faux pearls, of course. Janet could tell immediately. Small money, as Inocente said, and varnished plastic beads if one were to be cruel, but a necklace nevertheless and money he could ill afford.

For an instant Janet expected her new English acquaintance to be cruel and to laugh in the Spaniard's face. But Amanda appeared to have lost her piercing voice. It trembled quite feebly.

"*Gracias*," she said. "I don't know who you are, Pepe, but thank you. I will treasure this for the rest of my life."

Janet turned to leave but the woman with the pink hat reached out and held her arm. There was a mixture of sorrow, guilt and self-pity in those green, man-eating eyes of hers.

"Thank you for being so kind. I am so very sorry, my dear. Goodbye to you and this truly beautiful island."

More books by this author

The Skipping Verger and Other Tales

Another collection of charming short stories set on the island of Tenerife, from the hilarious and romantic adventures of British travellers to intrigue at the start of the Spanish Civil War. An English scientist meets a man with a strange walk. A Scottish artist falls in love with a passionate Spanish woman. Boys get up to mischief in the banana plantations. A British secret agent mysteriously disappears.

You can buy *The Skipping Verger and Other Tales* on Amazon.

ABOUT THE AUTHOR

John Reid Young was born in London's Welbeck Street in 1957. Although he has spent most of his life in the Canary Islands, home to his paternal ancestors since the middle of the 19th century, he was educated at private schools in England and Scotland. He joined the Royal Navy for a brief period in 1976 but admits to having entered the service as a rather immature schoolboy. Consequently it was a disaster. He worked for a subsidiary of G.K.N. in Shropshire before going to university where he read Law and Politics and completed his studies with a Master's degree in Diplomatic Studies. After a brief spell in London where he was interviewed for the SIS in 1988 he returned to the Canary Islands. He is now a family man where he has enjoyed nothing more than swimming in the Atlantic Ocean, playing tennis and gardening. He owns Tenerife Private Tours with which he finds great pleasure meeting people from all over the world. He has provided his voice to numerous recordings and has translated documents and publications for a variety of clients including the regional parliament. He has published several articles and keeps an historical blog, Travel Stories in Tenerife and the Canary Islands. His first collection of short stories, The Skipping Verger and Other Tales, confirmed his passion for telling a good story.

If you'd like to get in touch, please send a message to reidten@gmail.com with any comments, opinions, requests or general waffle.

Writing under an avocado tree I only get to talk to lizards and hoopoes, so any contact with the real world is much appreciated.